ALPHA'S EMBRACE

by

Wendy Rathbone

For Della, as always…

Chapter One

Misha

Thunk. Clunk. Bump.
That was Tracy on my right.
Shudder. Thud. Clank.
That was Cedric to my left.

I had lived with the sound of thumps on the walls for twenty years. That, and the howls.

I was used to it. I blocked them out when I wanted to. It was easy for me, having been raised here. This was normal. All of it in my white, weather-scratched castle by a green-slick pond I imagined was really an ocean full of pirates and serpents and mermen with seaweed hair.

My single, barred window, my ten by ten room, my very own metal sink and toilet, my narrow bed with the extra pillow I'd begged sweetly off a hall nurse named Donovan, all of it was my treasure by right, mine, owned and occupied by me.

I was rich. Lord of the beautiful and diamond-encrusted concrete lands protected by magic wire fences there to protect me and my realm. Of my lands, I knew all. I was able to survey them one hour each day and count the riches that sparkled in the hard ground.

It was a small kingdom, but it was mine.
Thunk. Rattle. Scrape.
Cedric moaned through the little hole in our wall, an aperture we'd spent a year creating when he was twelve and I was fourteen.

I ran to the hole. It was no bigger than my eye. I tried to peer into his room which was identical to my own except not as neat. Whatever belongings he had always ended up strewn on his floor: soap, toilet paper, toothbrush, pillow, sheets, mattress, his own white jumpsuit.

Once he told me, "The clothes, they hurt. They hurt, Misha. So bad."

He preferred that no clothes ever touch his skin. He hated sleeping on a mattress and usually curled up under his window or beneath his TV wall screen to sleep on his floor, even on the coldest days.

Now, as I looked through the hole, a brown eye met mine.

"Oh, so you are home," I heard him say.

I had not been out all day. My exercise hour was not until four p.m. Where else would I go but the showers in the mornings? But I answered him in careful measured tones.

"I am home, Sir Cedric. And the realm is at peace."

"You're always so quiet. Why are you always so quiet?"

It was true. I did not pound my walls like the others. I didn't scream, or moan or groan, or redecorate my room with my belongings tossed to the floor.

Sometimes I wanted to yell a lot. Sometimes when the heat of my skin became fire and I thought it was blistering and falling off, and when my cock stuck straight up hard as if to burst from my body, I wanted to scream. I wanted to throw myself against a wall. I wanted to die.

But mostly I read. I read everything I could on the tablet that was a gift to me from my regent who kept this realm in check for me until I was of age to inherit the crown.

The tablet was a purveyor of knowledge. It was my oracle. It could find and produce answers to my many questions. It and my television told me everything I wanted to know about worlds that were alien to my own, the worlds "out there" that were kingdoms with people different from me, with people called Alphas and Omegas.

Mine was the Sylph kingdom. One day, when I was ready, and the people outside were ready, we would meet. But I didn't worry about that too much. When or if it happened, the day would come. In my heart I knew it. But for the time being I was content to read all I could about them. About their lands and houses and cities, about their strange governments, their planes and cars and schools and stores, and their unusual matings.

"You're being silent again!" Cedric interrupted my thoughts.

"I'm quiet because I am doing a lot of reading," I told Cedric through the tiny hole.

"I don't know how you read," he said. "I tried once and it all mangled in my head. Words. So many words. I couldn't line them up right."

"I know," I said. "That's why sometimes I read to you."

"I do like that," he said. "But even so, it's so hard to focus. I need to get off. Get off. Get off."

His words referred to having an orgasm. Which we both wanted all the time. But you couldn't do it all the time or you'd rub yourself raw, or even break your cock.

When I turned fourteen, the sexual mania started for me. The heat inside my body began to rise like a molten liquid along with an urge to try to release it all the time. I had frenzied bouts of it, but it hurt when it got to be more than twenty orgasms a day. I taught myself how to calm my mind and to stretch each stroke session to several hours apart. At first it was agony, and reading helped distract me.

But poor Cedric couldn't control himself. He suffered a lot.

"Are you hard right now?" I asked Cedric.

"You are funny. So funny I would hit you if I could. I'm always hard."

I laughed. It was just a joke between us, really.

He was right, he was always hard. We both were. We rare, beautiful and valued Sylph princes who managed to live past puberty were hyper-sexual and knew very little respite from constant sexual arousal. It was one of the reasons we were kept apart and isolated one from the other. The realm could not

6

have men going about raping each other at whim, now, could it? Plus, Cedric's threat to hit me was not idle. Many Sylphs were quite violent, even the very youngest among us. Cedric had promised me many times over the years he might like to kill me if he could, just to see what it was like.

"Stand back from the hole and let me see," I commanded.

The brown eye vanished. I saw movement at the hole in darker shades. Those shades drew back and formed into a boy. An eighteen year old boy, two years younger than myself.

He was a pretty little thing with masses of dark, tangled hair that touched his buttocks, and a very skinny physique with olive skin. He was bony everywhere: his spine, his hips, his narrow shoulders, his knocking knees. He had a fierce but lovely face, exotic and angular and pointed, and if he held his chin high and stood still for once in his life, he was shockingly beautiful.

All Sylphs were insanely beautiful. I'd read that somewhere. Pretty and powerful in mesmerizing ways. But unfortunately, nearly all of us little princes didn't live long enough to gain our full power and become whole.

Cedric stood just far enough from the hole that I could see most of him along with the center of his room which was, as usual, a mess.

His cock stood out straight from his body, quivering.

My own under the thin material of my jumpsuit throbbed in response but I ignored it.

"Can you see me?" Cedric asked. "Can you see it?"

"I see you just fine." I laughed again.

"It hurts," he said, pouting, his dark pink lips protruding.

"I know, my lord prince, knight of the realm."

He stuck his tongue out. "You say such funny things. I'm not a knight or a prince."

"I say what I see," I replied.

"I can't touch it," he said. "I already got off ten times today. It hurts."

"Try to hold back."

He shook his head and his eyes rolled up. "I'm going to keep running into your wall until I fall."

"No, don't do that my beloved prince, my brother. I'll read you a story. Listen to me. Listen to my voice."

"I hate your voice," he said.

"You love my voice," I countered.

Quickly, I pulled up on my tablet a fairy tale romp I often read for comfort. I began. "Once upon a time there was a boy."

I heard a few thumps as I read, and I would pause and check through the hole. Sometimes I saw Cedric pacing back and forth before it, breathing fast. Sometimes I didn't see him at all and the thumps came rapid as his hands drummed the barrier between us.

But usually he sat naked in the center of his room on his pile of things and listened, his head low, his eyes closed.

It helped. For a little while, at least.

I read to him all afternoon and when I last peered through the hole I saw him curled up, his arms wrapped around himself, his wild dark eyes closed. His thin chest rose and fell. He'd fallen asleep.

And just in time, for I could hear the footsteps in the long hall. My servants were coming to take me to survey my realm.

Chapter Two

Geo

I'd only had my new job for two weeks and already my to-do list was piled high. How such a small institution could be fraught with so many problems mystified me.

My predecessor had been chief of staff here at Lakeside Colony for sixty years. It was obvious in his older years he'd let a lot of things slide. He'd been one hundred and seventy five when he left, long past retirement age. I wasn't entirely sure why he stayed on.

I was thirty, extremely young for such an appointment, but this colony was small, with only fifty-nine patients, all Sylphs, and out in the boonies. I was qualified as far as running a staff was concerned, but I didn't fit the protocols. I figured I got the job because, simply, no one else wanted it.

Looking over my daily to-do list, I sighed. I rang my assistant, Tory.

Tory came in with a put-out look and an Alpha's arrogance, as if I'd interrupted him from something important. He was older than I, and he'd been here ten years. So far we were stepping softly around each other, wary.

"I'd like to go over a few things with you."

"Do I need to take notes?" he asked. His face was hard, unreadable.

"No. Just sit."

He came in and closed the door.

I began to rattle off some things on the list I thought should have been taken care of by now.

"Why is that scum-infested pond out back not yet filled in and replanted with grass?" I asked. "There was an order for it over a year ago."

"There was a hold up," he replied. "I think it had to do with a permit."

"You think that's what it was? Or do you know?"

"It was turned over to the township last spring. They have been taking their time getting back to us."

"All right, then." My gaze trailed down the list. "What about the new beds. I see here fifty new ones are on back order, but that's been for six months. What happened?"

"Ah, we ordered those when we had a lice outbreak, but it turned out to be nothing. The patients really don't come into contact with each other, so it was contained. To be safe, we disinfected all the rooms, bleached the mattresses, and sprayed the patients. Problem solved. The money was allotted for other things, I guess."

"You guess?"

He nodded, looking bored.

I rattled off more problems and Tory had some trumped up excuse for them all. Broken windows never replaced. A part of the fence falling down in the back lot. A roof leak. Insufficient dumpsters for the amount of garbage the colony put out so that they were always overflowing, attracting flies, mice and rats.

From the outside, the place looked old but fairly all right. Inside, everything was ancient, but kept clean. However, looking over these papers and lists, honestly, it was a dump. I had my work cut out for me.

I understood the budgetary problems from day one. We had government subsidies and grants that kept the place running, but it was expensive, especially the in house clinic which operated like a full-on hospital. Some of the patients had extreme needs and required round the clock nursing. The majority were infants or children under twelve. The staff was large to manage their care and that cost money. When patients died and beds opened up, more patients were assigned to us.

10

Some years we were filled to capacity. Other years the colony grew quieter.

I had three Alpha doctors full time, a full staff of Alpha nurses and Alpha guards. I had a smaller staff of Omega cooks, janitors and secretaries to keep the place running smoothly. Everyone I employed was required to be mate-bonded which diminished the lure of the Sylphs, and the urge to give in to the older ones' seductive tendencies.

Misconduct remained at a minimum and our record cleanly showed that.

But I, as chief of staff, remained unbonded. It was completely outside protocol for working around Sylphs. But no one seemed to care. They had needed a new chief of staff and needed him now.

I had almost turned down the job because of that. It wasn't that I had loose morals or would ever take advantage of anyone who could not legally consent, but if a mate-bond was required by everyone in the institution, then I should have been bound by those same rules.

But for me, the situation was not clear cut. I still felt that fourteen-year-old, broken half-bond and the residual effects of its pull during my Burns. For fourteen years Mase had been bonded to another. He had been my first and only love. The Omega boy whose parents sold him at age eighteen to a rich Alpha in a foreign land.

My eyes still stung thinking about it.

We'd been best friends since I turned six and Mase was eight. Before I fully understood the meaning of genders and roles in our society, and how much he suffered because of them, I had imprinted on him. He was the home-schooled brother of a school-mate, and we met often at the riverbank behind my house to play the afternoons away.

Two years older than I, Mase was an Omega. To me it meant nothing. He was a person just like I was. He was the smartest boy I'd ever known, and the loveliest, and I looked up to him at every turn, following him about day after day.

But Mase had been promised to another. An arranged marriage, rare but legal. At eighteen he'd been shipped off.

We hadn't meant to begin a bond. We hadn't even known it was happening when I hit puberty and we started to fool around. Mase left when I was sixteen.

Though I wouldn't know the Burn until I was eighteen, those were the best days of my life. The purest of ecstasy ruled when I was with Mase.

Our parents knew we sometimes played together as children, but they never knew how close we really were. When it was discovered that a bond had begun, and we'd been practicing at having sex together as children often do, his parents wanted to sue mine. Mine wanted to sue his.

It got ugly.

They tore us apart and Mase was force-bonded to an Alpha far away. The bond I felt with him was ripped apart by that act, and the pain of it in my mind and heart nearly destroyed me. I didn't want to live without Mase. For a year I didn't talk. My parents sent me to the best doctors and therapists who told me I was an overly sensitive child and I was put on mood stabilizers for a year. Those were my darker times.

Eventually, my life resumed.

I never liked to think about that period in my life, or even admit to the pain inside that held me back from finding a full life as an Alpha, and from having a family.

Omegas at chattel farms had serviced me during my Burns, and they were all very sweet and submissive, but none had clicked for me and I knew it was at least partially due to Mase. Even now, I could still feel the ripple of him in my blood and mind. Due to that very devotion and loyalty which I'd admitted to on record for my required psych evaluations to get the job, protocols were eased in my case. My low sex drive was also taken into account. I was considered a non-liability.

Bringing myself out of my thoughts and back to the subject at hand, I glanced up at my assistant to continue our conversation.

"There is a budget allotment for cable, Wifi and game credits, but I see many of the rooms are not equipped. Why?" I asked Tory.

"Because those patients are either babies, or if older, have the mentality of infants. They cannot feed themselves. Music calms some of them, but it's a waste of resources to have the cable and TVs in those rooms."

"All right." My eyes scanned the list.

I knew the majority of Sylphs were born so severely handicapped they would not live past childhood. But I would never make the assumption until visiting them that they would not enjoy some entertainment.

"But you are sure the children who do have higher function are supplied with some outside stimulation?"

"It's the duty of the nurses to make such reports. I receive them and forward them to you."

I looked at my computer screen, clicking on my predecessor's inbox for the past year. It was sparse and did not take long to scroll through.

"I see no updated reports from within the last few months."

Tory took a deep breath. "Then I would suppose everything is in order."

"I would like to check on that myself."

The muscles of Tory's face hardened. "That might take a while."

"Why? There are fifty-nine patients. Half are infants. If I decide to interview the non-infants, at even three patients a day that would only take me ten days."

"Of course, sir. I'll set up a schedule. When would you like to start?"

"Tomorrow. And I will want another thorough tour of the building with a licensed inspector on hand. Please set that up for me as well."

"Yes, sir."

"And the groundskeepers. I would like meetings with each one of them, and afterward, I want a group meeting. I see there are three groundskeepers. That appears to be a very small number considering the acreage. And probably why the back of the estate has gone as wild as an abandoned graveyard. Has it always been this way?"

Tory shrugged. "I don't really know. In ten years, I only noted they kept the lawns trimmed out front, and the rose bushes. The back was always weeds. I think."

"Some of the rooms face in that direction. The view is not adequate."

"If I may be honest, sir, the view is the least concern of most of our patients. Sylphs, for the most part, don't even know where they are, let alone comprehend their daily routines."

"That is no excuse to have our establishment run into ruins."

Tory nodded. "I'll set up the meetings."

"All our patients have a range of varying needs. That does not mean we should expect their comfort is not lessened if we think they don't notice dirty sheets and windows, or a mass of tangled weeds in the yards. Or bland food that is the same each day."

"Some are on strict diets from doctor's orders."

"I understand. And some are not. But I will also be inspecting the kitchens. I've already looked over the menus and find them lacking in fresh fruits, salads and vegetables."

Tory looked as though he were suppressing another sigh. "The budget--"

"Is my problem," I finished for him. "I'll be rearranging a lot of it and asking for more from the state where we need it."

"Yes, sir."

There was a pause and Tory shifted nervously in his seat.

I watched him for a moment, then finally said, "That's all. Thank you."

As he left the room, I watched him shuffle across the floor. Did he hate his job? I understood if he didn't like me. I was new. It was to be expected. I was going to be making changes suited to my ideas of the smooth running of the colony. For people who had been working here many years, it would be seen as a disruption. But it all had to be done. I had five years of experience organizing hospital staffs and needs. It would all be put into play now.

I didn't like a lot of what I'd already seen in my first two weeks here and in examining all the reports. Too many reports, especially on patients, were lacking in detail that gave no picture whatsoever as to their individual health and well-being. There were no recent updates. Everything was too generalized, as if dashed off in a hurry.

I also didn't like it that patients had no contact with each other, no socialization. I understood Sylphs were violent, even the youngest children, and many could not even speak. Any who lived past puberty were hyper-sexual, but to never socialize with anyone except doctors, nurses or guards seemed wrong.

I would have to think on that issue and study it further, for I was no expert on Sylphs, by any means, but mainly a paper-pusher with a second degree in family therapy.

In the meantime, I had a lot of my own interviews and investigating to do. I'd be writing a lot of reports in the coming months, and doing a lot of begging for better funding.

When I took this job, I knew it wouldn't be paradise. I knew I would be working for the proper care of Sylphs, most of whom were extremely mentally handicapped. That alone would not be easy, but I wanted to try. The job paid well, and I knew I could handle it. I liked the idea of perhaps making life a little better for those who could not do for themselves.

It wasn't entirely altruistic. Of course I was getting paid. But I'd gone to school for this sort of job because I cared what happened to those people in our society who were hidden away, kept secret, including Omegas who should have more rights. I went to school to study the wrongs of the world and figure out how to right them. My save the world complex faded at the end of college, but I saw that I could still do good when I made my aims smaller and more focused.

I wasn't a real doctor, but I'd come up in the ranks doing tons of bureaucracy work in several hospitals, so I was qualified for the Riverside job.

I knew the doctors and nurses would resent me that I didn't have an MD, but I would work hard to make them see I was needed because of my organizational skills.

I was the guy who got things done.

Chapter Three

Misha

"It's cold outside. I have a sweater for you if you'd like," said my trusted servant, Laro, as he escorted me to oversee my outdoor lands.

My hands were cuffed behind me, but he would remove the bracelets as soon as I walked through the door to my realm so I could stretch in the fresh air, and play with the balls or the exercise equipment kept there for my use.

"Thank you, but I rarely feel the cold," I replied, smiling. Hyper-sexuality made my body feel hot all over. I was in a constant fever. But it was nice that he asked.

The sweater looked beautiful, though, a little old and lumpy, a little dusty, but I appreciated the fine wear my servants sometimes presented me.

My servants were good to me. They waited on me night and day, bringing my meals on antique golden trays, escorting me out into the hall—hands cuffed for my own safety—to stand against the gleaming walls while they changed my sheets and mopped my floor.

My floor was so pretty, a shiny brown color that, when wet, reflected deeper gold underneath. My clean sheets were daily crisp against my soft skin and smelled of the fresh lands I ruled, of far off winds and dusky seas, salt, tart… like tears of joy…the kind that leaked down my cheeks when I had so many orgasms I could no longer move my muscles.

The servants ran my baths for me, or let me shower myself every morning in a private room the color of the sea where the splashes of water echoed off the walls and the lights were startlingly bright. They always had clean towels for me, and clean white jumpsuits.

I was their little prince. I loved them all, and appreciated all the hard work they did to keep the castle going.

Laro's ring of keys jingled as he unlocked the outside door.

When I went through it, the air touched my face with a tinge of salt, smoke, and something faintly sweet.

"Do I smell flowers?" I asked as he unlocked my cuffs from behind me.

"More like something rotting," he said with a frown.

"Ah, no. I think flowers must be blooming somewhere. We just can't see them!"

"Hmm."

Laro went back through the door and closed it. I was left alone in the yard.

As a child, I had always played out on this pavement quite happily by myself, singing my songs, bouncing my basketball, or tossing a tennis ball against the stucco to teach myself how to catch.

Today, I went to the beautiful fence and touched the cold metal links, curling my fingers through the holes. I stared out at the green sea and the wild lands and up at the blue sky, and thought about how beautiful the world was. How lucky I was to be here.

When I was born, the doctor who delivered me named me Misha.

I never knew my Omega parents. Omegas were not allowed to keep their beautiful and rare Sylph babies. We were too special for them. We all earned exquisite treatment and care in beautiful castles made specifically for us.

One day, I looked up my name on my little tablet. Misha meant: Gift from God. So I looked up God. All that I read taught me God was like me, a lord over his lands, a lucky prince.

I was not only a gift from God, I was my own God. I knew ecstasy, compassion, and most of all, love. I loved everyone I'd ever met.

Granted, I had met very few people. But I loved every one of them, from the nurses who cared for me until I was six and was moved to my own luxurious room, to the servants who waited on me hand and foot, to the pirates in the little silver-green sea and the serpents who stirred within it. I even loved Cedric who so often said he wished I was dead, and in the next breath would beg me to use words to coax him to masturbation highs through the little hole in the wall between us.

But—I had never been *in* love. I wondered what that might feel like. I longed for it. I dreamed of it.

Today I made use of my time in the little yard with some weights in the far corner. It felt so excellent to stretch and use my muscles. This was the only time I had in fresh air to really move around. I could do exercises in my small room, but this was more fun.

My body had grown so much, and was so different from when I'd been a child. Of course I knew I was a man now, but for so long I'd been small. I swear I'd gained all my height and willowy stature in only the past couple of years. My thinness could not be helped, but I could make my limbs and stomach hard. I knew the routines. I loved the workouts.

Now at age twenty, my narrow body rippled with muscle, and I liked it. It was sexy. Even if I would never know a mate, I liked dreaming about one. I liked to know my body was at optimum health and fitness when I drew into myself and my fantasies of a prince waiting for his consort. A man waiting for his spouse.

The hour passed all too quickly. My hair was dampened from sweat, and hung in my eyes. I felt slick and hard and beautiful. It made me smile.

Laro returned to collect me.

"What are you smiling about?" he asked, wrinkles folding between his eyebrows.

"Ah, I just feel good."

He glanced at my crotch, then away as if he'd made a mistake.

Of course I was sporting an erection beneath my jumpsuit. I had very little reprieve from them. The servants always pretended not to notice. But they saw all. And I was not shy about it.

"You could have me if you wanted."

It was wrong for me to say such things. I knew it. But I couldn't help it.

I eyed Laro from the side, pretending it was no big deal. But how would it feel to have sex with another person? I'd been wanting it since I'd turned fourteen. And Laro—oh I loved Laro with his pretty bushy brow and his nose that hooked a bit at the tip. He was old and I liked that. He was amazing. Gray hair. What a color! I'd always wanted him, just like I'd always wanted my other servants. But none would have me for they were all mate-bonded. I didn't press the issue, but merely teased, for in the end I wasn't in love with any of them.

I wanted to be *in* love.

Laro puffed out some air and said, "Turn. Put your hands behind your back."

"No one would know." I kept my voice light and sweet. Innocent.

"Come along," he said gruffly.

"Is it because I am of royal descent? You need not be intimidated," I said. "We would simply be two men enjoying each other."

"You do realize I'm married," he said.

"You've told me many times." I grinned. "I'm so happy for you. You have a lover. A mate. I can only dream of it and it's amazing."

"It is amazing. And I'm sorry for your plight, Misha. But please stop asking."

"I meant no disrespect to your mate. I never mean to be a bother. I just feel so hot all the time."

"I know you don't mean it. And you're not a bother." He cleared his throat.

"The other princes are a bother, then." I did not ask it as a question because I knew.

"Always."

I nodded. "It's unfortunate, to be sure. But sometimes the royal blood runs too pure, and we as mere humans are not equipped to handle it. Our minds are fragile. We teeter on the edge and some of us, the most special ones of all, I think, topple over and fall."

"I'm sure that's true." Laro was the nicest of them all. He indulged me. He rarely lost his cool with me.

But through the pinhole leading to Cedric's room I'd often seen servants lose their tempers. Even Laro. Cedric was a difficult princeling. His fire burned and burned. He couldn't help himself. His thoughts flamed and his tantrums ruled and he had a violent streak. The staff were often forced to be rough with him.

Our usual walk back to my room bypassed halls with many doors to individual rooms. From within, I heard groans and heavy breathing, thumps and howls. Once in a while a door would be open with a servant or a nurse emerging. I stole quick peeks inside to see who was there. To put face and bodies to the noises I had heard for years.

Every room held a prince. They came in all shapes and sizes but most were small. Children. Once I saw a prince lying on a bed of blue, his hair so long it trailed off the pillow to the floor. He was made of all shades of golds and reds. He lay in slumber, so thin he was almost skeletal.

I asked Laro about him once. He told me that boy, Sari, slept nearly twenty hours a day and when he woke he was always in a daze. He could not function and required a lot of care. He could feed himself, but it wasn't enough. Several times a year he'd be taken to the infirmary for I.V. sustenance. He was thirteen.

Sari, the sleeping prince, reminded me of a fairy tale.

"Maybe he needs a good kiss to fully wake him," I had said.

Laro had answered with only a chuckle.

I could imagine full time sleep might be pleasurable if one's dreams were of ecstasy and paradise. There in your sleep-visions you could be yourself without the hindrance of a body that didn't quite work.

Today, through an open doorway, I saw a laughing child babbling in a language I didn't know, a crying boy, and a teenager who was jerking himself off so hard his cock was bright red. In that last case, two servants rushed from the room and the nearest guard said to them, "I already jacketed him once today."

The word jacketed chilled me. It meant you'd be fitted with a straight jacket and unable to touch yourself for the duration. Terrible!

We moved on.

While an Alpha didn't experience the Burn until age eighteen, Sylphs felt it at the onset of puberty. And it never let up.

Cedric was very hyper-sexual, but even he took breaks. Rarely did he have to be jacketed. And myself? I'd avoided the jacket. Lucky me. But the pain of always feeling the Burn didn't hurt any less. Simply, I had more control.

As we turned the corner to the hall where my room was, I saw the usual guard at the end. His shift went until late evening. At night, he would pace up and down the corridor keeping watch, though there was no way any of us were getting out of locked rooms. I liked to think he wasn't there to keep us in, but to keep others out—those who might come to do all the beautiful little princes harm, for the kingdom had its enemies though there was no overt war.

In addition to the guard, I saw two more men—both strangers—and one of the nurses dressed all in white. One stranger seemed to be exiting Cedric's room, or perhaps waiting to enter. The other stood a few feet away, leaning in a casual

22

slump against the corridor wall. He smelled different from the rest of them, more acrid, and I sensed his bond a wavering darkness.

With the first stranger, a sweetness wafted over me. I sensed no bond at all. This had never happened before, me seeing someone like this, sensing them so thoroughly, instantly wanting them on a level I couldn't describe.

My breath caught, for this unbonded stranger, this visitor, fairly glowed in the sodium lights reflecting off the beige, brick walls. His hair was made of a lot of brown colors merging at once and very straight. He had it sprayed back from his face, but strands from the front fell in single locks on either side of his forehead as if to frame the beauty of his face. His forehead was broad and tan, his cheeks full at the tops but tapered, and his jaw firm making his lovely pink mouth turn down in a slight but pretty frown.

When his eyes met mine I nearly swooned. I saw the lovely colors of the green pirate sea there, and deeper still, a solid kindness that would easily give over to strong determination, if necessary, to protect those around him.

His bearing communicated everything: straight back, broad shoulders, stance balanced and controlled. He was an Alpha, and a foreign king. No doubt about it.

My body responded in kind, telling me to submit. Not just as a prince to a higher title, but more. I wanted him as mine, and to be claimed as his in return.

The unbonded Alpha began to speak as if he'd been caught in mid-sentence before Laro and I came up. "And this would be--"

Ah, his voice, like slow, murmuring water, low and deep.

Instantly, I bowed. "Misha, Your Grace."

Softly, to the nurse who was looking at a tablet, the man said, "He's the eldest I've heard about?"

"Yes. The twenty-year-old, sir," said the nurse. "A first in the history of this establishment to live so long, I do believe."

"Is he able?" The king's eyebrows went up. "To do an interview?"

An interview? With me? No one ever came to visit me!

"Fully able," the nurse replied.

The king said, "I knew we had some of the rarer older ones, but I didn't realize he was so—uh—healthy."

"He has never been violent like the others. Not a day in his life," the nurse said.

I realized I knew the nurse who was talking. A distant memory from childhood came to me. He'd fed me and held me until I grew big enough to have my own room. I tried to remember his name. Prado. Or something like that.

"Let me see." The king grabbed the tablet from Prado. "And mentally?"

"Stable, sir. An I.Q. of 135 and that's without a proper education. Sylphs such as he are point one of a percent of the Sylph population, testing within all the normal human ranges, but he remains here because he is a Sylph and thus in a constant Burn."

The king looked up at me again.

I said to him with a smile, "You do know I can hear everything you are saying about me, Your Grace. I'm standing right here."

"I'm sorry. Misha is your name?"

I nodded.

He held out his beautiful hand. Blue-green veins mapped the back in such a pretty pattern I was almost dizzy. "My name is Geo. I'm the new chief of staff."

I bowed again. "I see that, Your Grace."

I did not take his hand. It was ungloved. And I was still cuffed.

His hand wasn't supposed to be ungloved. Everyone who deal with me wore gloves. But maybe he was special, different, and didn't need to wear the gloves.

Geo turned to the nurse with a raised eyebrow.

The nurse said quietly, "I assure you, he is not schizophrenic."

"May we talk in your room, then?" Geo asked, his hand falling as he turned toward my doorway.

"I would be honored to have you as a guest in my chamber," I said. "I am sorry I have no ability to offer you tea or coffee or a drink. You'll forgive me?"

"Nothing to forgive. I'm not thirsty anyway," he said kindly, indulging my silly manners, manners that meant nothing here, but who didn't like a little pretend?

Laro uncuffed me and the metal clinked as he fastened the cuffs back onto his belt.

As we entered my room, he said to Laro, "Leave the door open, please." Then to the nurse and the man leaning against the wall, he said, "Remain outside please."

"Bad idea," said the smirking man at the wall.

I wondered who he was. He didn't seem like a king, and certainly he should not be talking with such disrespect to one.

But Geo merely said, "We'll see, Tory."

"I'm sure you will," said Tory.

I smiled at the rude Alpha's statement. Maybe he was afraid for Geo. This was a foreign place for a visiting king. Plus, Geo was glove-less. But as I looked him over, I knew that Geo wasn't afraid of anything. He had a knightly look about him. He would not be one to test in combat.

We stood in the center of my room before I gestured to the bed. It was neatly made, as I liked it. "I use this as my couch. Will you sit, Your Grace?"

He looked down at it and his lower lip caught between his teeth. I took no offense. In fact, it made his mouth look even more delightful.

He sat and looked at me expectantly.

Immediately, I dropped to the floor at his feet, crossing my legs and leaning forward on my knees.

"Why do you call me Your Grace?" he asked.

"Ah. Yes. You are a king, are you not?" Perhaps he wanted to be addressed by another title?

"No."

"Chief, then," I decided. It might make him more comfortable. "You said so yourself. It is a synonym for king. I prefer king."

"You do? Hmm."

"Are you interviewing all the princes as you tour the castle?" I asked.

He blinked as if trying to make sense of me. I didn't mind. A culture clash was to be expected.

"Most of the—uh—princes here do not speak. Those who do have trouble articulating and focusing. But I am trying my best."

"Did you talk to Cedric yet?"

"I did. He is—interesting."

"Yes. He is."

"Misha, if I may ask--"

"You may ask me anything, Your Grace."

"Because of your talents and intelligence, are you given any extra things to do?"

"Like what?"

"Do you help out around here? Has anyone ever asked you to?"

I shook my head. "I am in isolation until the day I am ready to rule. And outside my room, I am cuffed."

"Ready to rule, you say?"

I nodded.

He frowned and it made his face even prettier. "What do you think this place is?"

"This place? Our castle, you mean? The realm? The green sea?"

"The green sea?"

"Yes." I glanced at the window. "You can see it from this very room!"

"The pond? Oh, we have plans to plow that over and plant a garden."

"What?" My chest constricted to think of the destruction of such a beautiful sea. "Why?"

"It is a breeding grounds for all sorts of viruses."

"I see." I folded my hands in front of me, squeezing. "But where will the mermen go? And the serpents?"

He cleared his throat and said softly, "There are other seas."

I smiled at his words. "That is true."

"Have you always spoken of this place as your castle and kingdom?"

"Since I was a child, yes."

"But you're no longer a child."

"No."

"But again I must ask, it is how you see?"

I smiled and my eyes warmed. "I'm not like the others."

He looked down at his tablet. "It has been noted."

"I have studied away my hours here. There is a learning game I have access to. Several, in fact. I have received online equivalents of a high school diploma and two college degrees from it. It's a game, I know, not real, but one of the degrees is in literature. It's very exciting. Watching television has also helped me learn my manners, and how to speak and behave around others."

"To do that all by yourself is quite an accomplishment."

"Thank you."

"You are doing very well. I didn't know many of these things about you. It's not in your records. But finding out is part of why I've now decided to learn more about you."

"Then you already know very quickly now I'm not a fool."

His eyebrows rose. "I never said you were."

"But you want to know why I see this place as I do. Let me ask you a question, Your Grace. If you were in my predicament, where the world was the breadth and length of your single room and the tiny yard out back to which you were allowed out once a day, how do you think that might feel to you?"

"It is a difficult life, I know."

"No. You work here, but you don't know. Not really. But humans can be very adaptable creatures. We have fantastic coping mechanisms. I know I do. I trained my eye to see the beauty in anything. It's like exercising a muscle. You get stronger every month, every year if you continue to do it. Now I see what I wish when I wish. It's a gift. I feel lucky."

"I would agree you have been very adaptable to the conditions of your life."

"Unlike my brothers here, I can reason and understand. I can open my tablet to worlds they cannot comprehend. I am very aware that most of them cannot even read, let alone speak. But I'm different. I have a lot of time to think, and to build my own world in my head. If you think that is strange, or an insane side effect of being a Sylph, I suppose that is fair. But it has kept me alive. And sane. For the most part."

He took a deep breath as though about to speak, then let it out in a slow whoosh.

"I see you are at a loss for words." I wanted to laugh.

"I didn't realize--" He stumbled over the words. "That maybe you shouldn't be here."

No one had ever said such words to me. It excited me. It also scared me a little for where else should I be?

"I suffer the Sylph Burn," I said. "As you probably well know, it can cause unpredictable chemical responses in the body. I have a perfect behavioral record, but I am still a Sylph. Your Grace, until I am of age and fit to rule, I cannot leave my chamber. It's for the safety of all, including myself."

"Who has told you this?" he asked.

"The last king—uh, chief of this great land. He spoke to me briefly two years ago."

"Hmm. I found no record of that."

"Probably because he had no clue where to categorize me in the files. I remember him being very uncomfortable with me, not like you, Your Grace, with your well mannered bearing. He wanted to drug me and take away my Wifi and not allow me to learn more, but some of the nurses came together on my behalf. I will always be grateful to them for helping him change his mind."

"But your record says you are medicated."

"It does? Well, unless it's put into my food, I know of no medications that I receive."

"Are you uncomfortable in your condition right now?"

"Are you referring to the Burn? Yes, it hurts. But there is no medication that is entirely effective against that for Sylphs, right?"

He nodded once.

"I've read that we have a tolerance against such sedatives. Cedric, however, is on medicine and he still needs constant orgasms just to soothe his misery. The medicines don't really help. The alternative would be to drug us into unconscious stupors."

"I meant, well, are you uncomfortable in other ways? Are your needs met?" He bounced a little on my couch—my bed. "Is this bed comfortable for you? And you are wearing only a thin jumpsuit, yet it's very cold outside. Do you have no other clothing?"

"I don't feel the cold, Your Grace. And my bed is luxurious and all mine. Do you see I have two pillows? We are partners. Companions, my bed and I. Plus, I am grateful to have my tablet and the TV screen in the wall."

I saw by the way his lips curved up at only the edges in a tentative smile that he was not quite as thrilled by all this as I was.

"Plus, there is a heating duct over there, see?" I pointed to the vent above the door frame. "It runs often at night. That's good for Cedric who often can't stand anything, even clothing and blankets, touching his skin. But truly, we Sylphs don't feel the cold like regular people."

"I see." Geo's eyes glanced about the room. He looked at the tablet he'd taken from my childhood nurse, Prado, who was waiting in the hall.

"Your profile here seems incomplete. Has anyone ever recommended a therapist?"

"Oh yes! I saw one once. I think I was twelve or so? I can't quite remember. But he decided I was not in need of more sessions at the time."

"I do see that in your records. But nothing since?"

"No, sir. Any doctor I have seen has recommended I need no extra benefits. I am not ill like the others."

"And no one has ever suggested that maybe you should have more time in the yard, or even help out for a few hours a day around the colony, since you are obviously able?"

"No. I am no trouble at all so nothing is ever said. And help out? I would probably unnerve the servants." However, the idea sounded good. I was often so bored.

Geo took a deep breath. The wrinkle between his eyebrows made him look so unhappy. But so handsome. I thought all beings were handsome, but this man was so smooth and fine he made my pulse race. And his hair. So straight and smooth with those dangles by his temples. If I touched his hair I thought it might feel like ribbon. I didn't get much chance to touch ribbon, but when I was a child I had a toy bear with a pink ribbon around its neck and I remembered stroking it over and over. The textile sensation calmed me; there was something safe about it, and about the pink tone which eased gently into my mind like caring, like peace.

I didn't know where that bear was. With another child now, maybe. I hoped so. I had not been allowed to bring the bear with me when I'd been transferred to my own domain. All children's toys were left in the children's area with the babies and toddlers. I was six when they moved me.

I blinked at the memory, my eyes warm.

"What were you thinking just now?" Geo asked.

"Oh, well!" I smiled and the blurriness of the room and Geo faded as my eyes cooled. "A bear I had when I was small. So long ago."

"A bear?"

"A toy they did not let me bring here."

The furrow at his brow smoothed but his mouth turned down. "Misha, I'm going to recommend a few changes for you here. Would that be okay?"

"Changes? Like what?" My muscles tensed, but I knew there was something about this interview with me he wasn't liking. My answers. My hospitality. Or maybe it was just me. I worried about very little in my life, but this concerned me.

"For a start, I want to see about giving you more of a life here. Not cooped up all the time."

"Oh."

Despite being bored a lot, his words filled me with apprehension. I didn't know what to think. This king had come into my realm and he wanted to change it all up. What if I didn't agree? What if the changes were too hard for me because of the Burn I felt all the time? But I knew I was strong. I could face anything, even pirates, I decided, if need be. Besides, I was a prince. I needed to stand tall. To show strength. I needed to be good for the good of all.

"I'll try," I replied, but I could already feel the weirdness of it. Would I have to be around people a lot? Wear gloves all the time? I wouldn't be able to orgasm at will while I was out of my room. It wasn't proper. I knew that. Would my intermittent erections make me stand out?

My face heated. I knew I would try for this king. This man. This Geo whom I already loved.

Chapter Four

Geo

He sat at my feet looking up at me and all I could think were single words: angel, gold. The light in here was too tarnished to do him justice.

Misha.

I wondered who had named him.

I wondered how he had slipped through the cracks so easily to be ignored and invisible when he wasn't sick and wasn't a problem for the nurses and guards.

But he was sick in that he was not quite normal. As a Sylph, he was feeling the Alpha Burn even now as we spoke. I could see he sat in such a way as to make his garment loose at the crotch and not show his erection.

I couldn't help but wonder if he would, at some point, make inappropriate sexual gestures, or outright proposition me. Many Sylphs who were able to articulate could not help themselves, and constantly attempted to seduce anyone they came into contact with. Sylphs such as Cedric, who lived next door to Misha. It was why the colony employed only mate-bonded workers.

But Misha maintained a polite manner and an even-tempered gaze. That kind of control was rare even for the sanest of Alphas during a Burn, and of course he was feeling that Burn right now.

What a beautiful and intelligent boy! But no, he wasn't a boy. He was a man. A very rare Sylph adult. Most never made it past early childhood.

Cedric was sixteen and suffering. His heart was giving out. He was the next oldest to Misha and unfortunately, the doctors said, would not outlast the year.

But Misha. What a wasted life! It wasn't right and despite the law, in the first moments as I began my interview with him, I vowed I would do all I could to break him out of this isolation. I didn't know what all that might entail, but it became a sudden project looming in my mind.

Just looking at him—I couldn't imagine anyone here not being impacted by him.

How could he have been so ignored? And yet, his reports were incomplete. No one spoke of him. No one had said a word to me on my tour of the patients to inform me that one patient in this colony would actually be able to intelligently dialog with me, understand me, and actively participate in his own rehabilitation.

What did they know that I didn't?

We talked for some time and he answered all my questions clearly and with a high spirit.

Toward the end of my interview with him, I said, "I want to see about giving you more of a life here. Not cooped up all the time."

"Oh," he said. "I'll try."

I had expected his reply to hold more energy and excitement. His eyes widened. He clasped his hands in front of his lap and squeezed until they were red at the knuckles.

I realized he'd been isolated for so long that this would have to be done gradually, in small steps.

"We'll go slowly," I assured him.

He swallowed, and at his lovely throat his Adam's apple bobbed. I had an urge to touch him there. I felt my body drawn to lean in toward him. He smelled like something forgotten from my childhood, sweet and lazy and secure memories apart from Mase, but stirring at the same time.

My cock gave a single throb as a tremor of warmth slipped through my abdomen.

A bonded Alpha might have responded the same, but his link to his Omega would have made him want to go home and have a nice time. I didn't have the luxury.

I would need to keep myself under firm control at all times around Misha. The tingles in my blood proved to me, even during my Burns, that my old partial bond with Mase was long gone, though I too often fantasized that some day he would return. I knew it was impossible, but my dreams remained.

In this case, my body responded to Misha. It was interesting to me that with Cedric, and the few others here who had made it to puberty, I had felt nothing. I had morals, of course, about underage leanings, and never experienced those leanings myself.

Sylphs in puberty gave off strong pheromones. Their age didn't matter. Those chemicals laced the air around them. The pheromones had Omega attributes but Alpha power, for the chemicals were pushed through their cells and skin by the constant Burn. It never ended for them. None of them could ever have been raised in normal families and households.

Still, I had felt nothing with them. But Misha was different.

As I tamped back my physical response to the beautiful man before me, I said, "Can you think of where you might like to start? For example, we can increase your exercise time."

"Yes. That would be very nice," he said. "I only have one hour a day right now. I do love the fresh air and sunlight."

His voice resonated through me, and caused another throb throughout my whole body. The accumulation of minutes in his presence caused a weird, sort of almost breakdown within me. As if my body were soaking up and storing his seductive air seeping through my careful barriers. I knew I needed to leave soon.

"Good. We'll start with twice a day, once a morning and once an afternoon."

"Thank you, Your Grace. May I also make a request?"

"Of course. And you can call me by my first name. Geo."

"Geo."

When he said my name, I wasn't prepared for the pleasant shiver that ran all over my skin. My nipples hardened under my shirt.

His lips opened for a breath. "May I see you again?" he asked.

He blinked. His eyelashes caught the hard light coming through his small, barred window. He was like a puppy with a longing gaze. For a dog, that look meant "pick me up" and "hold me." But for a man like Misha? I couldn't be sure. I didn't dare touch him even if I wanted only to comfort him.

I shouldn't have said yes to his request. I shouldn't have agreed to more meetings. He needed to be seen and cared for by bonded Alphas. He deserved more of a life, but he could not be out in public ever. It pained me to think that his rehab would be limited, for he was smart and sane and didn't deserve his plight.

So I said it. The one word I, as chief of staff, should have had more control over.

"Yes. I will visit again."

"Thank you." He looked so mild, his words completely polite and unassuming. Yet they held a power in them, just those two words, as if I had granted him the world and all the love it could hold.

It was very difficult for me to get up, to say goodbye, to walk out of that room and leave him standing there in that garish light, the door closing and locking behind me with a loud clunk. It was as if I were leaving something precious and innocent behind, something that needed me. Needed air and light and life and love.

All that I could not give him. Not in the ways he should have them.

Nurse Prado was waiting for me as I came into the hall, but as I glanced about I saw Tory had left.

"Tory said he had work to do," said Prado, noticing my gaze.

I sighed. Tory had come with me to many of my briefings of the patients, but he often complained. Several times I'd left him behind in the office to work. But I had wanted his views and feedback and had not thought it too much to ask him to accompany me as my assistant.

Misha had been the last on my list of patients to see for the day and I headed back to my office to file my reports and issue directives regarding Misha's case.

On my way past the nurse's station, Prado said, "Sir. I should also tell you that you should not have offered to shake his hand. It was a good thing he was cuffed. You weren't wearing any gloves!"

"Oh. I hadn't thought about that."

"It's protocol because of the pheromones secreted on their skin."

"I'll try to remember," I said as I walked toward the elevators. I didn't intend to touch Misha, but Prado didn't know that. The pheromones in the air were the true danger, and why only bonded staff was hired.

My arousal from being around him remained a mild distraction and I used the walk back to my office to control it.

When I arrived, Tory was at his desk in the outer office, typing away on his keyboard. I motioned him to follow me inside.

He came in and plopped himself in the chair before my desk, sprawling a little.

I decided not to say a word about him abandoning me upstairs.

"The case of Misha needs to be updated. He is isolated and he's an adult male with no mental illness and no physical limitations."

"But he has the Burn," Tory replied as if I were a child who knew nothing.

"So do lots of Alphas walking around in public right now."

"Well, they don't usually walk around in full Burns. They're busy fucking their mates, or buying an Omega's service," he argued.

36

"I understand he can't be outside in public. But he needs to gradually be allowed out within this institution. Not locked away. In fact, this institution is for extreme cases. I was thinking he might be able to be moved to a less strict facility."

"But he's a Sylph. All Sylphs are restricted to Sylph institutions."

"There are never exceptions?"

"None that I have ever heard of."

"Research this for me, will you? I want to know if there are rare cases like Misha. He is a citizen and he should have rights."

"Sylphs are less than Omegas. They have no rights."

"Omegas do have some rights. And Sylphs have the right to government care for the duration of their lives. The care should be compassionate. After all, we're not completely uncivilized," I said.

Tory smirked. "Not completely."

I didn't like his attitude, but I continued as if he'd not spoken. "Misha needs more mental stimulation than he's getting. He's smart and he has self-taught himself to read, to write, and converse. It's amazing, actually, and we are not serving him well by confining him."

"But it's a fact that Sylphs can't be trusted."

"That's a broad statement encompassing most Sylphs. But Misha--" I broke off and glanced at my window where I could see the muck of the pond Misha had called the Green Sea. "Misha is different than any Sylph I've ever heard or read about. Why wasn't this of any importance to my predecessor?"

"He usually didn't see patients. I believe he had met with Misha once, though."

"Well, I do see the patients, and I'm not going to ignore details that are inconvenient. For Misha, I want us to eventually get to a point where he's not locked away. He can care for himself. He should have an ability to move about, interact, and even help with the colony in some ways if he wishes."

"I think it's a bad idea."

"Why? We'd move forward slowly. We'd make rules."

Tory's mouth turned down. He sprawled a little in his chair, looking distinctly uncomfortable. "A lot of Alphas, despite their perfect mate-bonds, still have trouble. Not with most Sylphs, but with him. He's very alluring. It's a problem."

"So that is the reason to keep him locked up?"

"It is a very good reason. It's how we're trained to deal with any and all Sylphs."

"Well, I'm telling you, alluring or not, Misha deserves some freedom. When was it a crime to be pretty? Or in the Burn, for that matter?"

"If a Burn is unable to be controlled, Alphas lock themselves away until it's over."

"But Misha controls himself from what I've seen."

"From what you've seen."

"Do you have other information to the contrary?"

"No, sir." Tory glanced away.

"From now on, he's to get exercise twice a day. We'll move on from there, adding to his liberties, maybe, as we see how it goes."

"Yes, sir." But he did not look convinced.

"You're uncomfortable with this?"

"A Sylph running around is disconcerting. You are new here. You're not an expert on Sylphs yourself."

"No. But I do hold a degree in psychology."

"I know. A family therapist." He almost spit out that information, but I remained calm.

"And?"

"That's not specifically Sylph psychology," he countered.

"No."

He wouldn't look at me when he said, "You don't know about them. But I suppose if you want to do this for Misha you'll learn fast."

"About?"

"How they are. As I said, their allure."

"It sounds like you don't trust yourself," I challenged.

"I do." He swallowed hard. "I—I'm happily married. I love my Omega with all my heart." He nearly hissed when he said the word *Omega*. "But Sylphs have a reputation, like they're magical or something. People say they're bewitched."

"You should know better than that having worked here for so many years."

"I do, but the idea of it is on everyone's minds. All the time. And the ones in or past puberty do have a powerful allure. People say they can bewitch others. Even here."

"What people?"

He shrugged.

"Are we locking them away to keep us safe from them, or them from us?"

"Perhaps a bit of both."

I sighed. "All right, then. You're dismissed."

Tory sauntered out of the room.

He wasn't outright impolite to me, but something about him made me wonder if we were a good match, if we'd ever get along. I needed an assistant I could trust. Someone who would work with me, and not smirk so much. I didn't know everything, but I didn't need to be an expert to deal with the day to day paperwork of the colony. I had doctors and psychiatrists as experts to rely on. Their reports were crucial. The problem was Misha. His reports were outdated and incomplete. The last chief's record-keeping for the entire place from the past few years was abysmal.

Tory needed to understand that but I wasn't going to sit here and explain and defend myself to him. I didn't need to. I was the boss and I'd do what I thought appropriate with the expert guidance of my staff.

I spent the rest of the day working, but I could not get the image of Misha sitting at my feet looking up at me with such longing out of my mind. Everywhere I went, everything I did, that image haunted me. His golden curls. His honeyed scent. His beautifully noble jaw and straight nose, his eyes pale as a spring sky, his body long and lithe and tall, like a dancer. Like a ballerino. The quality about him that seemed to shift the air and affect my skin and my mind with electric pulses and maybe an impure thought or two wouldn't leave me.

I had strange urges to go back to his room and see him again. I tried to tell myself it was because I had a professional concern for him. That it was because I was curious and needed more information to update his files. That continued isolation into adulthood would damage him mentally beyond repair.

In truth, I wanted to look at him again. My mind craved it. His beauty and his plight. My body wanted him. How shallow could I be? I'd looked upon beauty before and not been obsessed. I sated my Burns with gorgeous, wonderful Omegas who treated me well. But nothing made me think of or want them beyond that. I always thought it was because of Mase. Because of my broken heart.

But Misha somehow circumvented all that.

A tiny voice in the back of my mind said: *It's just the Burn.*

I wasn't scheduled for another Burn for four weeks. My body had a rhythm I could rely on. My Burns came every two months on the nose. I was never late or early. I did not have strong urges in between Burns. I had been around Alphas about to go into their own Burn and never been affected. Most Alphas did not respond to another Alpha's Burn anyway, except to get out of their way if they happened to be between them and the Omega they had eyes for.

Sometimes Alphas took each other as lovers and though it was seen as not ideal, it was legal. But the Burn mostly affected Omegas who became instantly aroused around the Alphas who needed them.

No. I wasn't in the Burn. But I was obviously affected by Misha's constant Burn. But not like an Alpha to an Alpha. He was a Sylph. Something entirely different.

Sylphs had no Omega wombs or egg sacks. I thought of them as another sort of Alpha, but with damaged DNA.

History bore my thoughts out. Before taking this job, what little I'd read in books about Sylphs of the past said they were monstrous warnings from the gods. Sylphs were what Alphas might become if they did not control themselves, if their Burns ruled them. They were called anti-Alphas by some sects, and through the centuries they usually did not survive long, and those who lived to reach puberty were feared, isolated, or ritually killed.

It was also said Sylphs had no ability to bond. But what Sylph had lived long enough to even try?

Meeting Misha had derailed all my expectations. Had he somehow tricked me? Was that why his files were incomplete? Did others fear his demeanor as a trick as well? It made sense in an odd way, for if true, no one wanted to be the one individual who fell for his tricks and lost their job, or worse.

I remembered a rhyme from childhood about Sylphs.

Take a Sylph to bed,
Tomorrow wake up dead.

But rumors had their way of twisting the truth. Beliefs that were never challenged ended up hurting innocent individuals. Omegas knew this firsthand, and groups for Omega rights had waged huge uphill battles only to fail again and again.

I didn't know what to think anymore except I knew in my heart that Misha was being wronged.

In the next weeks we'd see if the little freedoms I planned to give him backfired or not. It was a risk, but for his life, I felt it was worth it.

Chapter Five

Misha

I automatically placed my hands behind my back and waited for the cuffs. When they didn't come, I turned to see the two guards watching me, waiting to see what I would do.

There were two guards this time, not one as was the usual routine.

I had been in my same routine for so long, I'd forgotten for those few seconds of exiting my room that King Geo had granted me freedom to walk the hall unencumbered.

Out here in the corridor I could hear the screams and thumpings a lot louder. I heard Cedric pounding at his walls and pictured his poor little fists bloody and raw. I wished I could go to him, but the rule was I could move about the colony but I was not allowed to see other Sylphs, only the staff, the doctors, and the other workers. And hopefully Geo himself.

I heard one guard whisper to the other, "I still think this is a mistake."

I pretended not to hear.

I was allowed to walk the entire floor unencumbered, though the two guards trailed me at every instant.

The floor wasn't huge. There was one long corridor and two veering off in the middle left to right, forming a plus sign. The screams up and down those corridors were normal. I'd always heard them. But today I felt apart, distant, not one of them anymore, and so they wrapped about me in a distinctly eerie atmosphere.

The elevators were right by the nurses' station. The stairs were to the right of that. Usually, when I was taken to my one hour a day exercise, we used the elevator.

Today I went to the elevator and I myself pushed the *down* button. We all took it downstairs to the yard.

The guards opened the door to the fenced-in area and this time they left it open. They did not lock me in. They did not accompany me, either. They simply stood chatting outside my view and let me do as I pleased.

It had started to rain, so I finished working out fast and sat against the side of the wall under the roof overhang, letting the mist wash my face. The beauty of the world, all grays mixed with the wet green of the lawn and the green sea I could see beyond it encompassed me. The blacktop before me shone like polished onyx. I felt like I was encased in a jewel, a prince under a spell waiting and waiting.

When I had enough of the cold air and damp, I moved through the door on my own, watching the guards glance up as I entered.

I ran my hand over my hair, shoving the raindrops off, tossing the wet curls. They said nothing to me but I could scent and feel their undivided interest: metallic, warm, melting.

It felt so weird to be free to walk anywhere and they simply followed. Like good knights trailing their prince to keep him safe from assassins and the like. Knights with big hard-ons they were trying to ignore.

I didn't know where to go. A strange feeling of paranoia swept me at the idea that I had to make a decision. It prickled my skin. I knew I was strong, and a prince, but my body began to shake. I was hard, always aroused, and though I'd masturbated twice in the morning, it had not alleviated my tension as it usually did for at least a couple hours.

I could see no other option but to go back to my room where everything was settled and calm.

We went up in the elevator and I said nothing, when normally I was somewhat verbally expressive. I could hear the Alpha guards breathing and feel their heat at my back. In my hypersensitivity, I again smelled their musk and spicy scents.

43

Guards, nurses, everyone—even the Omegas who delivered my meals—were aroused from dealing with me, their cocks expressing interest in my Sylph scent, which I knew was like candy to them. They couldn't help it. I was used to it. But feeling free now to do as I pleased, the sensation that I affected them all in this way changed for me, as if it had become my responsibility now, my burden.

The mental change of going from total lockdown to freedom in both mind and body, the idea that I could walk about, my room's door left open if I wanted it, caused a fit of conscience in me. I was a Sylph. It was my fault if they felt things they didn't want to feel because of my existence.

I wasn't sure how to process that.

As I walked by the nurses' station I brought up my courage to say hello. They knew me and I knew them. The Alphas there acknowledged me with nods and stifled hellos, but that was all. They kept darting nervous looks at my unbound hands. It was odd, I knew, not to be cuffed. Though I'd never been violent, again, it was the idea that I had a freedom to be more like one of them that unnerved everyone, for they didn't trust me. Not at all. The fact was, I wasn't one of them. I was far from it.

Labels. No way around them. I was what I was.

Screams echoed up and down the corridors. I had a sudden urge to join my fellow Sylphs. Throw back my head and let out a loud howl. But I kept my head down and my voice to myself.

I tried to walk slowly back to my door and not show I was eager to be back inside in my territory, a place I'd known to be safe.

When I got there, I turned without a word and shut my door behind me. I did not hear the familiar lock slip into place. It should have been wonderful. It was only odd.

My body shivered, chilled from the rain and cold weather, but I did not feel it. I burned deep inside, a coiling, growing pyre of flame that constantly licked my veins and sent surges of adrenaline through my cells. My blood was always hot. My cock relaxed only after an orgasmic surge and that did not last long.

I peeled off my damp jumpsuit, looking at my skin as I did so. It was glowing, pink tinged with gold, and my cock bounced up when it was free of the confines of the clothing, pink-tipped and wet, the shaft darker than the rest of my body, filled with blood.

How often I had wished for consciousness to be the center of me, my mind and my dreams and not my cock. My beautiful thoughts. But they weren't. My cock was the center of my being. It ruled me like an angry child dictator. It demanded my attention.

I loved the pleasure it gave, no argument there. I basked in orgasmic splendor many times a day. But sometimes I wanted to stop. Just stop. The fevers. The fog of them, and the heat that cascaded over me until I thought I'd surely burn up.

I craved a whole day where I never thought once about jerking off. A day where I didn't have to think about the tension and all the ways I used to alleviate it.

Medication didn't work. The worst of us were sometimes sedated, but that didn't stop the flames that leapt over us. It didn't stop the priapism, the constant hypersexual erections that actually became painful.

I lay back on my bed enjoying the coolness of my skin in contrast to the inner fires of my body. I tried to relax, staring up at the gray ceiling, faded in places, and cracked in one corner.

I touched myself lightly, my cock firm against my belly, and ran my fingertips up and down the underside. It was wonderful, but I didn't rush. I never rushed. I hated taking myself too quickly to the brink because I would often lose control and chafe myself from too much stimulation. Going too fast never helped, and my cock would remain hard and wanting but hurt when I tried to relieve it.

Cedric had this problem and would never listen to me no matter how softly and insistently I tried to teach him how to give himself better pleasure. It was one of the reasons he howled and screamed into the nights until the nurses came running and sedated him into an uncomfortable doze. Using extreme doses needed for Sylph metabolism took its toll, and still did nothing for the Burn.

On the other side of me, Tracy, who made loud thumps all the time, also probably got sedation, but I couldn't be sure. I didn't know him. We had no peephole in the wall between our rooms. I'd never seen him. I only knew his name because I'd heard the nurses sometimes call out to him.

The younger, prepubescent Slyphs also screamed a lot, but they were in more emotional pain, not sexual. Not being fully developed, they suffered from various madnesses all of which were frightening, and all of which I was grateful had somehow skipped me.

I stroked myself lightly over and over until my skin all over my body tingled and I calmed despite my arousal. It was soothing for me to play the game with myself of how long I could hold out before coming. I had learned this trick early on after suffering in early puberty when all I wanted was orgasm after orgasm. I had learned quickly it hurt too much to make orgasms my only goal.

I seduced myself. I pretended with myself that every time was my first time, that I was a shy virgin who wasn't sure he wanted to give in too easily to such deep and overwhelming desires. The game never worked well for Cedric, but it did for me.

My other hand skimmed my chest and ribs, palm down, and the skin on skin contact produced warmth and chills at the same time. I got lost in sensation. The room filled with the scent of sex which to me was sweet and earthy at the same time, like flowers drenched in tart rain. I loved it.

I wished I had a mirror so I could see myself. I had a dim mirror over my small sink. It was dark and showed me blurred images of myself—enough so I could comb my curls and see

46

that I even *had* curls, and wash my face. I did not shave as most Alphas and Omegas did. I had never managed to grow a beard.

I was pretty. I knew it. I had strong features, and my hair did not stick out but hung in sweet circles about my head, loose and long, below my ears. The curls felt like satin to the touch. My face was clear and my eyes a very pale, sky blue. I liked myself. I did. I wished I could have a partner, a real partner like a mate. A bondmate. But Sylphs did not bond. We did not have Omega parts, and we did not knot like Alphas.

Often, I wished for a knot. From what I'd read about them, they were pinnacles of ecstasy. An Alpha trait to be envied.

Omegas could take knots up their backsides and be in ecstasy because of all the erogenous zones within their rectums. I wanted that, too. But I wasn't an Omega. I never would be either Alpha or Omega, and I would never have a mate.

Today, I fantasized about Geo as I touched myself. Geo who wouldn't leave my thoughts. Geo who I wanted more than anyone I'd ever met. Instant love, I told myself. As it was with everyone I met. But something about him made me feel my lusts deeper, stronger.

He was beautiful. I discovered long ago that everyone I met was beautiful and worthy of my love, but this—it was different. Geo had taken my attention like none of them. Maybe it was that he'd talked to me like a real person, listened and asked questions. That was, of course, flattering.

None of the guards or nurses did that—talked to me or flattered me—beyond what they had to say to me to let me know what was going on around me. But really, I'd never had conversations with them. Cedric was the person I'd come the closest to having actual conversations with, but those were short since he had trouble focusing, or making any real sense most of the time.

As I lay back, I heard Cedric calling, but I ignored him.

Geo was my central focus right now. His lovely full lips, his straight locks of hair that framed his bare forehead, his eyes the color of the grand sea that glimmered and glistened outside my window. He had tanned skin a few shades darker than mine, and broad shoulders. He wasn't much taller than I, but it felt like it because his Alpha bearing and presence made him big. So big and full.

I wanted him. I wanted him to touch me and stroke me and kiss me. Oh, what would it be like if he sucked me? I had never experienced such a thing, and longed to feel it—a mouth on my cock with the wet pull of a suck and a greedy tongue doing all sorts of incredible things to my cock head, fluttering, licking, sipping.

My cock throbbed beneath my fingers. I reached at the space between the head of my bed and the wall to grab my lube. I poured its coolness into my hand and finally took my cock gently in hand, wrapping my fingers about the swollen shaft, spreading the substance all over it.

Everything inside me flamed.

I began to move my hand up and down. I was skillful at this after so many years alone with my own rampant disease of constant arousal. Unlike Cedric, who lost himself in the pure agonies of lust until he could not think or reason, I kept my awareness. I knew the path, well-worn but never old, and delighted in the details along the way.

My room took on a deeper fog in the haze of my rising ecstasy. I heard rain on the window mixing with the thumps on Tracy's wall and the cries of Cedric through the tiny hole in his wall.

In my mind I saw Geo standing by a beautiful sea with crashing waves, and the salt wind blew his hair back in a lovely brown wave. He wore black pants and a white shirt that billowed a bit between the elbows and shoulders. His pretty pink lips were smiling. At me.

I could see by the way his pants fit that he wanted me, that he needed me, and his hand beckoned as he stepped into the shadow of a sandy cliff. I went to him and he reached out.

His heat permeated the air. He was in the Burn and I responded to that with a rush of blood that jerked through my whole body. I almost came before he ever touched me.

Then I felt his arms. An Alpha's embrace I'd craved my whole life. I'd been held as a child but not past age six. I no longer remembered the exact mechanics of it, but the comfort of a hug was something I craved every day. And I had a great imagination.

"My prince," he whispered into my ear.

In my fantasy, the hug was tight and intimate. His cheek pressed mine. Our jaws rubbed together. His hand on my back moved up and down and our chests met, our knees bumped, our cocks strained together against the clothes we wore.

An imagined hug. Dual arousal. A smile and a whispered acknowledgment of who I was to him, a prince. My love. My personal bondmate. That was all it took.

My slick hand squeezed my cock and I came hard, feeling the hot spatters of my own storm, my personal rain on my stomach and ribs and chest.

I tossed my head back and forth as the pleasure coursed through me, enfolding and encompassing me like a blanket, the strokes of a hundred hands, or that one hug I'd always wanted.

For those moments I knew real peace. True happiness. As if the world were made for me and I for it. A magical place where I fit, where I was normal, where I could live.

Geo faded from my mind and I blinked away the tears. Happiness. Joy. And for the first time, worry and anxiety.

I was no longer behind a locked door. The door was open but I had nothing to do or give yet. No being. No ability to make a life. To interact with others. I was still a prisoner inside and always would be.

A knock came. At first I thought it was Tracy, who still thumped—his foot, his head?—against the wall. When it came again, I sat up. The sound had come from my door.

Who would knock? Everyone here came in without warning.

I looked at my jumpsuit still drying, draped across the sink, and realized I couldn't put it back on just yet. I grabbed a thin blanket from my bed, wrapped myself, and pulled open the door.

Geo stood before me. From my dreams.

He wore exactly what I'd envisioned: white shirt, black trousers. His hair was a single wave back from his forehead with loose strands at the sides. His eyebrows rose when he saw me naked in nothing but my blanket. He looked a bit confused.

"Where are your clothes?" His gaze swept the room.

"Wet from the rain. I was outside earlier."

"You should have spare outfits. I will certainly have more brought to you."

They weren't outfits, they were more like uniforms. But I said nothing to contradict him. I didn't care about clothes, only why he was here. It was wonderful to have him visit, but why had he come? Why had he arrived at mere moments after my orgasm in his dream arms? Certainly as a visiting king he had much more to occupy him than a silly prince.

I wanted to make him mine. A determination in me to do so welled up, and only my conscience held me back.

Geo responded with a slight shiver as if he'd read my thoughts, but he seemed to ignore it. Maybe he'd only taken a deep breath. Maybe seeing him standing in my room was still all my imagination.

He turned at my open door and spoke to someone outside it. Then he glanced about my room again, surveying my bed and the rumpled blankets. Last time, it had been neatly made, as I always kept it when I wasn't using it. But now he had to know. I'd been lying naked upon it when he arrived. As observant as he was, I knew he couldn't come to any other conclusion. I could still feel the semen drying on my chest and my body flushed to think of it there with him in such close proximity. I was sure he could smell it on me.

He cleared his throat and looked at me.

I stood in the middle of the room holding the blanket closed across the front of my body.

"I came to check in on you. To see how you're doing after the new liberties that have been given to you," Geo said.

"I went for a walk but the guards followed."

"They are there simply to see that you are safe."

"Would I be in danger?" But I knew as a Sylph my allure was strong. Like a siren call. Irresistible. Online stories confirmed it. My own behavior confirmed it. I wanted Geo like no other. I wanted to drop my blanket right here, right now and seduce him.

He shook his head *no* but I saw in his green eyes a hesitation. "Everyone is mate-bonded who works here. So in that capacity, you will be left alone."

"Except you."

He blinked. "What?"

"Except you," I repeated. "You're single."

"How do you know?"

"A citrus scent mixed with something earthier but clean. Unless you're wearing some cologne, perhaps?"

"You can smell my mate-bond status?"

I shrugged. "I can. The others, they are more muted to me, like how fall smells before a rain, the fields dying but it's still lovely. All lovely."

"I can smell mate-bond status only with Omegas," he said. "And not one hundred percent correctly all the time."

"I can smell it on both. There was one the other day that was different, though."

"Who?"

"The Alpha who was with you when you came to interview me. Your assistant, maybe?"

"Tory?"

"If Tory is your assistant, then yes. That one."

"What do you mean he is different?"

"I don't know. He doesn't smell like you, though." Not as delicious, I wanted to say. "But also different from the others who are mate-bonded."

"But Tory is a bonded Alpha."

"I don't know why he's different, then."

I couldn't take my eyes off him. In all the vids and pictures online I'd viewed I'd never seen an Alpha I wanted more than Geo. It was the Alphas who attracted me, both on my tablet and scented in person. I'd seen Omegas and never had the same reaction.

Though I could smell that Geo was unbonded, there was an underlying scent of a bonding I couldn't place. When we'd first met, I hadn't sensed it. Or maybe I had sense it but thought it was interference from the others around him. Then I had a flash of insight. "Were you bonded before?"

His whole body moved back. "Not exactly."

"That is an unusual answer," I said.

"Yes. I suppose you could say I was almost bonded, a partial connection had started, but that never came to be."

I watched his eyes darken.

"I'm sorry." My whole body hurt to think of Geo so sad for so long.

"No need. It was a long time ago."

I smiled. "Long time ago? You're not that old."

The light from my doorway darkened and one of the nurses I'd said hello to on my walk came in with two folded jumpsuits. He set them on my bed.

"Thank you." I looked up at Geo. "You just now ordered them? These extra clean clothes for me?"

"Until I can get you other attire, it's what's on hand."

"Other attire? I'm sure these are of fine quality. Perfect. But I do like what you wear. Your white shirts. And you wore a tie the first time I saw you. I should some day like to own a tie and a white shirt."

"Misha." His tone deepened.

I looked up from the clothes, holding my blanket tighter around me. I needed a shower before putting on a clean jumpsuit.

"I am making a series of reports. I think you should be informed."

"About what?"

"About you."

"Oh."

"Normally, in facilities that house Sylphs, this isn't an issue. But having met you, if you were anywhere else in any other condition I would recommend release for you. You aren't sick and you need not be held against your will. You would have some rights."

"But I am not anywhere else. I am here. I understand my plight."

I had never had conversations like this with anyone, not even the friendliest of nurses. Everyone stayed away from me. They did their duties and stayed far away. Royalty and intimidation went hand in hand.

"It's wrong and I want you to know I'll be advocating for more freedoms for you. Not just from your room, but maybe outings away from this facility. You deserve a life. The doctors have told me there is no reason you can't live a long and normal life of two hundred years. You have a strong heart. You have many Alpha qualities. You are smart. You could—and should—have a life."

My cock responded to his voice, bouncing up. I loved how he praised me. How could I not want him and love him because of his caring for me? His attention?

Everything I was yearned toward him. But he was talking as if I would participate in all these changes by myself. It frightened me. Would he be there?

I looked up at him, putting all my desire and pleading into my gaze.

I saw him wobble a bit, as if he were responding to my allure, but he remained strong.

"Haven't you ever dreamed of more for yourself?" he asked.

I had, yes, but only in my fantasies. What would he think of me if I told him the truth? That I was not meant for the world. That I needed to wait longer and was not yet of age to rule.

My lungs jerked in a moment of unusual fear. Normally I felt safe in my life, if lonely. The walls and locks and routines gave me a sense of security. I'd known nothing else. What was Geo saying?

"I would not ask so much leeway for myself." My voice came out hesitant. "I am not uncomfortable here. You need not worry."

"I know it's a big step. Of course it would be a gradual move. But maybe you could even be taken to another institution, one centered on rehabilitation, with more freedoms."

Was he crazy? I couldn't be in proximity with just anyone. Even the bonded nurses, doctors and guards who were around me wore protective gloves all the time. I couldn't be free. Not ever!

I'd never felt such shock and fear at a simple statement. But it wasn't simple at all.

I went cold inside. For a moment I couldn't speak. All thought left me. All language and sensation and identity. All that was left was a dark hole and I was in it.

I was made of echoes, all the voices of my confined past spinning and bouncing off the bleak, black walls of my awareness, whispering about danger, shouting warnings.

I never felt cold but now I had ice in my veins. My body seemed to quake. I felt pressure, warm and firm, against the middle of my back. A strong arm. A hand in the darkness appearing before me.

What was left of me still had enough capacity to know it was Geo. Gentle Geo who had taken an interest in me. Who thought he was helping me. Who was at this very moment reaching to catch me with his ungloved hands because I was definitely falling. Why were his hands ungloved yet again? Didn't he realize his error? Or maybe he had never had any intention to touch me.

"Misha. Misha."

I heard my name as if from far away. I'd dropped the blanket. I'd wanted him to see me naked. I wanted him to want me. But not now. This was an accident.

I could feel him—the crispness of his sleeves against my bare skin, the buttons at his chest pressing my side, the warmth of him seeping through all his pretty garments to mingle with my sudden chill.

The Burn inside me, quiet for the moment in the face of my fear, threatened to return. So much contact with another person, something I hadn't had since I was a child, overwhelmed all my senses.

I tried to open my eyes, tried to see through the darkness. My body spun and became very light, and I realized he'd lifted me into his arms at the same time he called for a nurse.

It threw me off even more, my equilibrium shot, adrenaline rushing through my system. I wanted Geo and I couldn't have him. I was a non-being, invisible to the world, a captive prince in a realm of shadows. I had denied it in my fantasy life, but it was true. I was a monster who could never leave his lair. Didn't Geo know this? Wasn't he the expert in charge?

I squirmed to try to get away, but he held me tight. He shouldn't be touching me. I wanted it, but he shouldn't. He shouldn't.

My inner voices, the ones based in abject fear, grew louder.

He doesn't mean to rescue you at all; he's throwing you away.

He will toss you to the streets and the Alphas who roam them for prey.

You will wander alone until you starve and die.

My heart pounded. I could not get enough air. The darkness deepened and finally the voices faded along with the whole wide world.

The last thing I remembered was the sensation of arms holding me aloft and a voice saying, "Hold on, now, Misha. Hold on."

Chapter Six

Geo

"Nurse, a little help here!"

I saw Misha's eyes roll back. His body began to shake. He looked like he was having a seizure and I reached out to catch him as he fell. His thin blanket piled at our feet. He swayed into me, naked—so beautifully naked—and when my palms touched his skin he was cold and shivering.

Before I realized what I was doing, I'd picked him up and his head lolled against my chest, his left arm dangling.

It was wrong, I knew. I had no gloves. I was being reckless. But honestly, I'd had no intent to touch him. And now, other than recognizing his beauty and allure, I felt fine. I really did.

I pulled him tight to me and headed fast for the door. In the corridor, two nurses met me.

"Why didn't you put him on his bed?" one asked.

"I'm taking him to the hospital wing downstairs." But of course they were right. I should have set him down, called for the doctors and waited.

The one who questioned my intent touched Misha's face with a gloved hand, pulling his eyelids up and listening to his breathing.

"He's just fainted and he's a bit cool to the touch." He stood back, eyeing me up and down with disapproval.

It was against protocol to touch a Sylph even gloved unless one was a doctor, nurse or caregiver. People were afraid of the pheromones produced by their skin. But they were the same ones that were in the air. So I wasn't too worried.

However, I should not have been so casual about the rules. What was wrong with me?

I took a step forward but both Alpha nurses blocked me.

"Sir, he can recover just fine in his room."

"I've changed my mind. I'm taking him to the bathing room. Hot water will bring him round." I hadn't thought of it until I spoke. His body still shivered in my arms. I knew a bath would help and I wanted to care for him. His reaction to my ideas of change for his life were my fault.

When the nurses kept staring, I said, "Move."

They stepped to the side. I watched them glance at each other, but they didn't say another word. As I moved forward with Misha in my arms, I felt them staring at my back as I made my way down the corridor to the showers and bathing area.

My mind swirled. What was I doing? Why was I avoiding the protocols? I pushed those thoughts away. Instead, my more compassionate thoughts took precedence. Misha was a real person. Misha was not a normal Sylph. Misha was just like the rest of us, but had never been given the chance to prove it.

My dominant Alpha came to the forefront. Brash and bold. I'd never felt quite like this before. It was wonderful to feel so confident about my decisions. To be in charge and not have to face questions.

A guard stared at me as I walked by but he said nothing, and when I glared at him he glanced away.

The bathroom had light blue tile walls and several high windows that let in natural light. Two shower stalls stood to the left. Further in, another alcove opened up to more tile, and two large, white bathtubs.

Misha was moaning a little, coming to as I set him in one tub and turned on the water. Testing it, I balanced hot and cold until it was nice and warm, and plugged the drain.

Misha leaned back on the cold ceramic, moving his arms up a bit. His eyelids fluttered. The warm water flowed all about his hips and thighs. His bent knees parted revealing his beautiful body even more to me, inner thighs long and lean, skin looking soft as flower petals. Hip bones dented the edges of the muscled skin of his abdomen. Waves of muscles ran up to the curve of his ribs. The tight balls were lightly dusted with pale blond hair. And a rosy cock, ample, sweetly soft for now, had a pale pink tip peeking from the foreskin. It started to bob as the water level rose.

I couldn't look away from him. He mesmerized me. Hypnotized me. My body responded to him as if he were an Omega and not a Sylph in a constant Burn. Thoughts filled my mind. Desires. Forbidden lusts. I wanted to touch him in more than a medicinal manner. I wanted to take him, the urge as strong as if he had a womb I could fill with my own seed to make a baby.

I never thought about babies. Never. But with Misha I irrationally wanted to mate him until he conceived. He wasn't an Omega. He didn't have a womb. What was I thinking?

His scent washed over me sweet as rain, as fields newly blooming, as a spring wind. My cock grew harder in my trousers. I could control this, I was convinced of it. But it felt so delicious. So natural.

Quickly, I sprinkled bath salts and bubble bath into the water surrounding him. Both would drench his scent for the moment, as well as hide his body from my unsteady gaze.

I had been professional in all my jobs my whole life. I wasn't hyper-sexed. I knew dealing with Sylphs would be a job different from what I was used to, but I had no notion at the time I took the position as chief of staff that I'd ever meet a Sylph like Misha.

I thought they'd all be sick. I thought they'd all be children.

When Misha's pale blue eyes opened, he jerked a bit, momentarily confused.

I rested my left hand on his shoulder. More ungloved touching. I knew better, but I couldn't stop my instinctive responses to comfort a man who had done nothing wrong in his life except to be born neither Alpha nor Omega. The Burn he felt daily was not his fault.

"It's all right. You fainted. And your temperature is down. The bath will help warm you."

He blinked up at me. "You brought me here?"

"I did." My answer seemed all wrong because it should have been a nurse attending him. Anyone but me.

I realized how strange it all was. My usual well-ordered thoughts had vanished. I couldn't think. I still wasn't thinking even now as I grabbed a cloth and soaped it, pressing it to his chest.

Misha put both hands on the sides of the tub and sat up straighter, the water and bubbles spreading over his abdomen and thighs and rising. He glanced about.

"No nurses? Just you?" His eyes seemed to bulge when he saw my bare hands.

I took a breath but didn't answer as I smoothed the cloth over his chest and gently rubbed.

"Just me."

"Geo. Thank you. That is a very generous gesture. But you don't have to. I can bathe myself."

Our eyes met. His lips curved into a gentle smile.

"You scared me. I was worried."

He gulped. His voice came out soft and wondering. "No one has ever cared for me like this."

"Surely the nurses are efficient."

"They are," he said, looking down at the cloth. "But they rarely touch me."

His tone had a depth in it of distance and echoes. Loneliness.

"Geo, you are very kind," he said softly. "I have never known such as you. You are a good king. But probably you should leave now." He stumbled over those last words, as if maybe he didn't want to say them aloud.

"I am no king."

"No?" He looked so young as he asked the question, so pure and new and uninformed. He'd never been in the world. What was I thinking to tell him I would advocate for his release? It would terrify anyone who had spent their life locked away. It would be like learning to walk and breathe all over again. But sometimes learning new things hurt.

I moved the wet, soapy cloth over his shoulders. He leaned into the touch and my cock throbbed.

"I'm sorry if I scared you with my plan," I said.

He hunched a bit in the water, letting his hands and forearms slip underneath the steaming liquid.

"You don't need to be sorry."

"I can be over-zealous when I get a task I think worthy of completion."

"Am I a task?"

The question forced me to back up again, to reassess everything. "You are a person. Real and alive."

My hands slipped a little off the cloth and onto the smooth skin above his pecs. Heat raced over every inch of my body, trembling every hair from my calves to my nape. My eyes went hot. My cock strained against its fabric cage. I was responding to the touch, nothing more, I told myself.

"I confess," he said, meeting my gaze and holding it. "I was a bit frightened at your words. Frightened for myself. Frightened for others, even though I have never felt a dark thought toward another in my life. But I am afraid of what others might think of me, or do to me. A Sylph loose in society? Even with a chaperone? Has it ever happened?"

Of course he was afraid. How could I be so stupid? It'd sprung all my ideas about helping him too quickly. I had not thought ahead. My impulses had caused him pain and in turn, that pained me.

"There have never seen Sylphs outside institutions to my knowledge," I replied. "But surely somewhere in time it's occurred."

"Hmm," he said. "You really think so?"

No. I didn't. But I wanted him to believe it.

"My kingdom isn't ready for me, I think," he said.

I wanted to chuckle. I felt so comfortable with him. But I kept my emotions to myself and said, "Perhaps not."

"I wouldn't want to be a burden to anyone. I think I can rule from here and be just fine."

He spoke it as a statement, flat and decided.

"With the doors unlocked," I added.

Slowly, he nodded but seemed unsure.

"I might not feel entirely safe," Misha said. "Even with guards. You say all your Alphas who work here are bonded. But I've seen the ways they look when they think I don't notice. I'm not normal. They can't see me as normal, so how can I expect strangers in the world to see me any other way? I don't think I could ever rule from anywhere but here."

He was right and I wasn't thinking straight. I wasn't thinking at all.

My hand slipped to other parts of his body now. Down and across to one leg, the cloth smoothing over his beautiful golden skin. The white bubbles clothed him all over, sparkling in the rays of sunlight from overhead, glistening in rainbows from the yellow lights on the walls.

How could he be even more beautiful than he already was? The water lapped against his muscles and the white suds made his skin gleam. His leanness was amplified by the water and the shine of it on him.

I had a sudden urge to taste him. Immediately, I wanted him more than I'd ever wanted anything in my life.

He looked up suddenly and tilted his head. He had already told me I should leave, that he could bathe himself. I expected him to make the statement again. He should have asked me why I was bathing him when he could bathe himself. But he didn't say another word.

Could he smell my arousal? Did he know?

A part of my mind teased me with Sylph fantasies, children's stories, really, that they could read minds. That they

62

were part fairy, part Alpha, and might steal bad children in the night and raise them up to be their mates, never discerning between Alpha and Omega, loving both equally.

I wasn't a child, but he was whisking me away already and he hadn't done a thing.

I, however, had broken probably fifteen different rules of this establishment in one afternoon.

I didn't care, but why?

My hand continued with the cloth, bathing him like I would a beloved.

Everything in me was turned toward him, all senses, all attention, all yearning. The myth of fated mates came to me. True mates. I wanted to laugh at myself. But with everything I was experiencing, how could I deny it?

"Geo." he said. Just my name. Nothing else. But in that single word was contained all his unasked questions. All his innocence. And all his burning.

His cock bobbed up out of the water. Not his fault. He couldn't help it. I didn't dare think it might be for me, not truly, for he would respond to any touch. It was the way of the Burn. I knew it firsthand when I had my Burns and craved the caress of any Omega, or any touch, really. Warm. Soft. Tight. Wet.

He was responding because I was the one present in the room, but not necessarily to *me*.

Still, I wanted him.

I brought my hand up out of the water, the cloth dripping upon the spectrum of bubbles on his right thigh, sending tiny cascades of soapy liquid down the soft skin. I couldn't look away. I wanted to look at him forever—for the rest of my life.

I had to leave now!

I handed him the cloth and grabbed the rim of the tub as I stood and turned away. "I'll go get you a robe."

It was a delay tactic, an excuse not to leave. My own mind was manipulating me.

"Geo," he said.

I froze in mid-step.

"Thank you."

When I returned with the robe from the area closet, I re-entered the room just as he was standing, all the water flowing over him, clusters of bubbles still present on his legs and arms and chest.

With perfect balance, he stepped from the tub. His hair was darker from the water, and wet all the way through as if he'd dunked himself. His long curls turned to tangles that reached for his shoulders, spreading more moisture. Strands stuck to his forehead. His cheeks were pink, his eyes like blue lights, his lips slightly parted.

By all the gods that ever were, I needed all my strength now, for I could think of only one thing: I wanted to grab him hard, carry him off, and make him mine. It was a primitive brain response. Alphas who were out of control and labeled dangerous often fell victim to it. I never had. Not even with Mase. But with Mase, we were both so young. I had not yet experienced the Burn. We never knew that more adult level of need and connection between us.

But right now, this was like nothing I'd ever felt outside the Burn.

I draped the robe on a bench that ran the length of one wall, and then had to hold my hands behind my back, tightly clasped, to keep from reaching out to him.

Grab. Hold. That was all I could think. *Take. Take. Mine. Mine!*

What was wrong with me? He was a Sylph, that was what was wrong with me. He had this affect.

No wonder no one touched him. No wonder he said what he had about not feeling safe. Not from himself, but from others. Even the bonded ones had given him discomforting looks. He had told me all this. Had I not heard him?

I was too busy fighting the pull. The magnetism. I realized that only now, and yet still I denied it.

You're stronger than this, I told myself. He's a patient. Like a child.

But Misha, standing naked before me, was no child.

I wanted to advocate for his rights. For his life. But after all this—and I should have known after our first meeting, though I'd been in denial as to my response—I knew he could never go out into the world. Not the way he was.

We barely knew each other and here I was harboring dangerous thoughts of carrying him off, hiding him forever, having my way with him.

I was acting like a dangerous Alpha!

I turned away again.

I heard him walk toward me. Or maybe it was wishful thinking. I wanted him to approach. To reach out to me. But that could not happen.

By the gods, this should not have happened. I should never have taken this job. Only Alpha arrogance made me think I could be immune. Why? Just because I'd once had a tiny inkling of a bond as a teen? How could I be so stupid?

I took a step toward the door.

I heard a rustle of cloth. He had found the towels on the rack, fresh for today. He had found his robe. I could hear him and I wanted to take those towels and that robe and rub him all over with them, and then with my hands, my mouth, my tongue.

My balls ached.

"Geo."

I wanted to tell him not to say my name again. I never liked my name. But out of his mouth, it sounded like a fancy endearment, intimate and cajoling. Filled to bursting with desperate hunger.

"Do you need to go back to your office?" he asked.

My back to him, I replied, "Yes."

"Can I see your office?"

"Maybe another day. I have a lot of work to do." No! That wasn't what I wanted. I needed him to come with me. To my office and everywhere I went from now on. I wanted to take him over the desk, and against the window that faced the eastern mountain range that turned purple at sunset. I want to possess him in the dim light of my office corners, and on the black rug that lay right before the doorway. I wanted him bent over and in my mouth all at the same time. I needed to put my cock in his every orifice. I would knot him in the mouth, and in the firm grip of his ass. I wanted nothing more than to own him.

This was so wrong!

I forced my legs to move. Away from the bathing room. Away from him.

I heard him say my name one more time. Almost a whisper.

That tone swam through the air toward me, curved its way through my skin and into me, settling on my heart.

I had no memory of how I made it to the hall, but I spoke to the two guards there.

"Allow him to go where he wishes. Make sure he comes to no harm."

Then I fled.

When I got to my office reception area, Tory started to stand and speak.

I said, "Not now."

I nearly crashed through my door, closed it behind me and locked it. My breaths came deep and long. My muscles screamed at the tension. My cock strained for release.

I rushed through to my private bathroom, unfastened my pants, and at the first touch of my hand to my shaft, came hard, aiming as best I could for the toilet.

My head fell back. With my free hand, I grabbed the sink for balance.

Gods, I was burning by the time I was finished. But I wasn't in the Burn.

I'd never responded this way to any Omega even when in the Burn. I'd never come with a single touch like that. Never.

I always needed more friction no matter how desperate or hard or burning up.

When I finally re-oriented myself, I made myself clean and unwrinkled, and presentable. I left the bathroom, went straight to my desk and sat there for about an hour. Not working. Not doing anything. Just sitting and ignoring my calls, my messages, my texts.

The air seemed too close, too thick. I was breathing fine but I never felt as if I got enough oxygen.

Finally, I turned to my work. The day was growing later, and darker with the storm. I was behind on everything, so I planned to stay late.

With every move I made, every report I read or forwarded, or signed off on, I couldn't stop thinking about Misha.

When Tory came by my door to say he was leaving for home, I had barely noticed the time. I merely nodded to him, and continued on with messages, reports and files—everything I had put off to the side to deal with later, I dealt with. I made myself into a machine and got the work done.

The next time I looked up, the time was nine o'clock.

I realized I needed to get a meal, go home, and get some sleep. But for all these hours, all my needs eluded me. I shut everything down in my body.

Now my stomach growled loud enough to echo in the room. I was more thirsty than I could ever remember being. But still I sat. I stared for long minutes at my closed door.

I was afraid to get up and go anywhere in the building for fear of running into Misha. I could still smell him on my hands, though I'd washed them over and over again. I was being ridiculous and I knew it but I couldn't stop the fear, or the rush of excitement that I might see him. That maybe I really wanted to see him.

Forcing myself to rise, my muscles aching from too long in the chair, I hastily made sure my desk was in order and opened the door to my office.

Tory's desk sat empty and silent, his computer off. Beyond his alcove I heard the night staff making their rounds. Footsteps. Echoes of soft voices. And more distantly, a cry now and again of a patient.

I had met all the patients. Even the older ones, Tracy and Cedric, had no affect on me. But I had not talked with either of them, let alone touched them. They were incapable of any focus, or an ability to be interviewed.

But Misha. How was I to know?

They should have hired a doctor, an expert, for this job. It was a lot of paper-pushing, but as a general family counselor, I was out of my league here and I knew it. All because of one adult patient.

I made it out of the building without seeing or speaking to anyone. The night shift was thin and so they stayed busy.

After a stop for a to-go burger, I got home and crawled into my bed with my food and turned on a movie with the sound loud.

I ate without thinking, without tasting. I heard the TV but didn't pay attention to the plot. Everything was a jumble in my mind. Tired and exasperated with myself, I finally fell asleep.

Chapter Seven

Misha

There were no windows in the castle corridor, but when I went to the end of the hall, the natural light fell about me in white rays so brilliant I could see the floating dust particles in the air. The sight made me smile.

It had been two days since King Geo left me in the shower area alone. I had not seen him.

I knew why. He was embarrassed. He'd gotten an erection when he tended to me. It wasn't his fault. It was mine. I didn't mean to faint, but I wanted him to touch me. I wanted it with all my being.

Having read a lot about my condition and what my Sylph label meant to the outside realms beyond our lands and holdings, I expected Geo to respond to me. I intended it, though I never wished to hurt or burden him. Erections didn't embarrass me. Every day I had them too often to count.

But King Geo seemed very uncomfortable. I didn't like that it might mean he would stay away from me now. He was the only one who spoke to me as if I were an actual person. He was the only one in my entire existence who'd shown any interest in providing a better life for me with my current surroundings. He had given me attention. He had tried to see me for me.

I had only met him twice, but I couldn't stop thinking about him. I wanted to see him again. But what if he didn't want to see me?

I promised myself that if I saw him again, I would consciously try to hold back my allure. I would be standoffish and casual. If possible.

I kept replaying in my mind what had happened in the showers by the bathtub. He'd touched me. First he'd used a cloth in the soapy water, but his fingers had slipped a little and connected with my chest, shoulders, stomach and thighs.

Skin to skin contact. I'd never had it in my life. When the Omega caregivers and Alpha nurses who'd cared for me when I was very young held me, they always wore protective gloves. They never held me for long, even when I cried. It taught me very quickly how to self-soothe.

What Geo had done for me after I fainted had been unprecedented. He didn't act like a nurse toward me. And he didn't wear gloves.

In all my quiet studies alone in my room, I'd read about skin on skin contact between Sylphs with Alphas or Omegas. Most of the stories were fairy tales about bonds being unwillingly formed. But I had read other research that said Sylphs couldn't bond. But how could anyone know? Sylphs did not live long enough to find out. Well, none of them had met me. And stories were only stories. Fables. No one could know the truth for certain. So they all operated based on fear.

We lived as if we were infected. A touch to my back by a guard steering me toward the exercise area, or taking my cuffs on and off, was never skin to skin. Never. They all kept their bodies covered head to toe, showing only their faces. The only naked body other than my own I'd ever seen was beautiful, feral Cedric through the hole in our wall.

Over and over I tried to analyze that moment when Geo's bare fingers slid against my wet skin.

I'd felt the familiar tingles of my body, and the usual allure, but that wasn't abnormal for me. My arousals were frequent and not necessarily inspired by anything. But with Geo, my king, of course I felt something more. He was special; he was different. Jolts of pleasure had coursed through my body and I could not control my erection. I had become fully hard in seconds from that touch, which had been only innocent and helpful.

70

But my body hadn't known that. My breath got stuck in my throat. My skin heated up fast, hotter than the warm water he'd been using to bathe me. Added to that, the sensation in my chest and stomach created a great tension. It was almost like fear, but surrounded by cascades of pleasure. I had wanted to lurch forward and grab him as if I were falling. I had wanted to hold onto him. Curl into him. Never let go.

Certainly, I loved everyone I met unconditionally. But I had never had the urge before to leap into their arms and claw into them as if to make them mine. I had never felt passion toward another, or such great urgency.

Now, every time I took a breath an empty hole seemed to open up in my chest. I couldn't breathe deep enough. One thought of him and the air would expand in my lungs, feeding me, but it wasn't enough.

Last night, before I went to sleep, I'd felt tears fall down my face into my hair. My pillow grew damp. I didn't know why I was crying. But Geo kept smiling at me in my mind, and I kept crying.

Now I wandered up and down the halls, unshackled. The nurses had gotten used to me. They said hello to me, but only if I spoke first. My two guards followed me around, switching out for new guards at the ends of their shifts.

I wore my usual jumpsuit and the robe over it, the robe Geo had given me, though I wasn't cold.

I came to the elevator and activated it. I was allowed on the first two floors of the castle. The first floor held the king's greeting room. The room he called his office.

Today I decided to go there. If King Geo would not return to me, I'd go to him.

A map to the first floor offices greeted me on the wall outside the elevator doors. I had never been down here before. But I knew how to read well, and I immediately saw the office number for Georgio Barrister. Geo. It had to be him. And what a beautiful name!

I turned to my guards. "Suite 111. Which direction?"

"This way," said one in a low voice.

I led them to the door with the correct number. The door had a glass window in the middle and through it I saw a room with beige carpet, a big window and a desk.

An Alpha man sat at the desk. I'd seen him once before. He'd been with Geo on our first meeting but had refused to come into my room. It was Tory, the Alpha who had the strange bond scent.

I opened the door.

Tory looked up. His dark eyebrows rose as he saw me. His chair, which was on tiny wheels, slid back several inches on a plastic square over the carpet, and his hands gripped the armrests. His body went taut.

I smiled at him and bowed. "My lord."

When I came up from the bow he remained frozen to his chair, the surprised expression on his face never wavering.

"I have come to see King Geo. I'm sorry I do not have an appointment. Is he available?"

"I—uh—don't think you're supposed to be here."

"The king has proclaimed I have access to floors one and two of the castle," I said. "I assumed that meant here as well."

"All right." The Alpha leaned forward in his chair and picked up a phone. He pressed a button on the base. In a low voice, he said, "He's here." A pause. "That one. You know. The adult Sylph." Another pause. "I forgot his name. Yes. I will."

As Tory looked at me and started to speak, a door at the end of the room opened.

Geo stood in the archway and my heart began to pound as I saw him. After not seeing him for two days, he was like a breath of fresh air to me. So handsome, his hair scattered to the sides of his forehead in brown streaks, his eyes like the green sea, and his white shirt fitted tight at his broad shoulders and chest, tapering to his slim waist and the black belt of his pants.

All of me wanted to surge toward him but I remained where I was.

"Misha." He said my name with a sort of wind behind the softness of its pronunciation.

My skin began to tingle. In addition to the fever of my Burn, my skin heated even more.

"Your Grace." I bowed to him. "I came to visit. I hope that is allowed?"

He did not answer yes right away, which caused a slice of pain through my chest. But I forced myself to stand and breathe, stand and breathe.

"Misha. Of course." He paused, looking momentarily uncomfortable.

I read everything into that pause: want, guilt, pain, compassion, shame, fascination. I wasn't psychic. I was simply used to all the reactions both Alphas and Omegas had toward me.

But this Alpha, King Geo, caused all the same responses in me. That was the unusual part. With Geo I experienced everything at once. The shame and guilt came only because I could see in his eyes a respectful nervousness now, and I didn't like it. I wanted him to be all right with me. I wanted him to like me as he had seemed to during our first meeting, and never have to be on guard.

It couldn't happen. What I wanted and what was reality were two different things. I didn't kid myself. I wasn't a prince and he wasn't a king. I wanted him and he wanted me. But I was taboo for him.

I knew these facts. I never wanted to hurt another, or be a burden. I worried often about the position I put others in because I wasn't normal. Yet still, here I was.

Geo stood in his doorway a moment too long before saying, "Would you like to come in?"

"Yes."

I forced myself not to hurry forward. My robe brushed along the hard, beige carpet of the outside office as I strode toward him.

He turned aside and ushered me in. Out the corner of my eye I saw him gesture to my guards to wait outside.

I glanced around the fine room. The wall that faced his big window reflected light with its white coat of paint. The other walls comforted the air in a soft yellowy-beige. His desk was huge and made of the prettiest, honey-colored wood. On it he had two computer screens, a keyboard, and various items like pens and notepaper, a purple ball the size of my fist that looked like real amethyst, and a white coffee cup with a picture of a snoozing cartoon bear on it.

His desk chair was dark blue and had a large, cushioned back. In front of his desk sat two plush chairs, also blue.

"You have a beautiful space," I exclaimed.

"Thank you." Stiff. Formal.

He started to shut the door, but before I heard the clasp catch, he stopped it and left it open about half an inch. He pretended nonchalance, but I could see his every move was checked and careful.

I didn't like it one bit. I wanted to return to that feeling I'd had in the tub when his hands had caressed me without a plan, when he had taken care of me through instinct and not logic, not because he was forced.

"Are you enjoying your newfound freedoms?" he asked.

So formal, again. Like a king.

"Yes." I ran my hand along the back of one of the plush chairs. "I missed you."

He frowned and approached his desk, moving around it to his chair. "You did?"

"I thought you might visit me again. I had hoped." My body fought me. My Burn wanted me to touch him. It took all my strength to hold back.

"I have been very busy lately." Voice dry, hoarse.

"I understand. You have important work." I offered my best smile.

He gestured to one of his chairs. "Would you like to sit? Would you like coffee?"

Before I had a chance to answer, he went to a small table against one wall where I saw a coffee pot. He poured some of the dark, steaming liquid into a white cup and turned halfway in profile.

"Do you take cream and sugar?"

"I probably do, though I've never had coffee before."

Now looking at me straight on, his left eyebrow rose. "No?"

"They don't give us coffee, or any other stimulants for our meals. Water, juice. Nothing hot, though I've always wanted to try."

"I see. I should not have presumed." He set the coffee pot down and took a step toward the door. "I'll be back in one moment."

I sat and stared about the space again, trying to learn what I could about Geo from it. The décor was sparse, but I liked that. His coat hung on a hanger on a hook by the door. Black. Short. I saw a brown leather briefcase sitting on the table by the coffee pot. He probably carried his laptop in it.

Not much else in the room was informative as to his nature or history. But I knew a lot already. He'd revealed himself. He'd told me in a few words of his tragedy. His love for a boy. His partial bond broken.

I took a deep breath just as I heard his footfalls and he came back into the room.

"I just checked in person with Doctor Prim. You can have coffee. It's simply not a part of a Sylph's normal diet."

Ah, but I wasn't a normal Sylph. I knew it already, but I didn't like to think of myself as abnormal, either. I wanted to be as normal as possible. As an Alpha. Or as an Omega.

He handed me a steaming cup of the dark liquid. Slowly, I took a sip. It burned my lips a bit but I took a little of it into my mouth and it coated my tongue with a semi-bittersweet flavor tinged with fire.

Geo crossed his arms, still standing by the side of his desk. "You like it?"

"Yes."

The cup warmed my palm. I wasn't cold but it was a comforting feeling. Like a soothing caress.

"Thank you," I said.

"Did you want to see me about anything specific?" Geo went behind his desk again, and sat facing me.

I thought about that word. *Specific.* Yes. I came here because of something specific. I came here because of Geo and how he made me feel. Because I missed him. Because more than my physical body yearned for him. It was core-deep in me, this sense of longing. I'd never had it so strong before. As if I'd come apart and die if I didn't feed that longing.

How could I say these things to Geo? He was the king. It was taboo if he ever thought of me as more than a Sylph-prince of the castle.

I knew he did think of me as more. I'd felt it in the bathtub. I'd seen evidence in his response, in the line of his erection through his pants.

I decided to lie.

"No. I was just curious where you worked. And you've been the kindest person to me in the past week. I wanted to tell you. To thank you."

His eyes half-closed as he smiled at me, as if to both accept me and shut me out at the same time.

"You're welcome."

"I appreciate that you're advocating for me."

"I am. But I have hit some snags."

"Oh." My heart flipped in my chest.

"Rehabilitation, for one. You have never been outside these walls. You would have no ability to survive on your own. You'd need a sponsor at the very least. But worse than that, you are a Sylph. I can't find any records of a Sylph living free and whole in society. It just doesn't happen. If you go out, you will not be a danger to others, as would most Sylphs who cannot control their emotions and behaviors. But you would be in

76

danger. So rehabilitation at this point with that as a goal is on hold."

"I'd be in danger from other Alphas, yes, I tried to tell you that before."

He frowned as if he didn't understand me. "There is a pheromone all Sylphs produce that spreads into the air. In children it is to lure another into caring for him, feeding him, seeing to his needs. But as an adult it is much more than that."

"I know all this," I said. I wasn't bored, but my low tone might have conveyed otherwise.

"Yes. So did I. But I had hoped there might be a way to suppress that for you. Disguise it. I'm still looking into that, but nothing so far."

"You mean through drugs?"

He nodded. "Or outside interference. Such as colognes that might act as filters."

"I understand. It is impossible, of course, that I could ever live outside these walls without some assistance. And my guards." I tilted my chin down and eyed him with all the humor I could manage. I added, "I am, after all, a prince."

I could read him well through all my senses. He smelled withdrawn and nervous, which came across like a bite of pepper, not bad but with a sting.

My skin went hot and cold in his presence, and that told me he was sending out his own pheromones. I didn't feel that with others at any given moment. With him it communicated a constant desire. In his voice I heard it as well. A deep resonance, not flat the way nurses and doctors communicated to me, but layered with nuances of emotion. The thickness of more than just lust.

It was easy to read him. He wanted me as I wanted him, and on more than a level of simple allure. It caught at his core, too, as it did mine.

Maybe it was because he was unbonded. I wasn't sure. But none of the responses from others here in the castle were like Geo's.

In my own case, I'd had a sense like I was dying for the past two days. Now in his presence that anxiety level vanished.

I wanted to tell him everything about all my thoughts. I wanted no secrets from him. How to start? I cleared my throat.

"I want a field trip with you."

He made no move except to blink.

One step at a time. "Maybe just a walk outside the fence at first?"

"You want me to go with you?"

"I trust you. I know you'd let nothing bad happen."

"I really can't. I have work. I'll assign it to your guards."

I lowered my gaze to the amethyst ball sitting on his desk, shiny and perfect and cold like the earth. "You shouldn't have touched me in the bath."

He pushed his chair back a little, his eyes widening at my bluntness. "Misha, I thought you'd had a seizure!"

"And you took care of me."

"An instinct, that's all. I'm sorry if I made you uncomfortable."

"Instincts. I have them, too. You touched me." I lowered my voice to a whisper. "Skin on skin. Why weren't you gloved? I can't forget that. It didn't make me uncomfortable, but I can't forget it."

He rocked back in his chair. "I wasn't planning on what happened, you fainting. You scared me. I didn't think. I acted."

"But now?"

He didn't reply.

"You feel it, too, though, right?" I pushed. "You can't forget."

Still, he said nothing.

"I think I might die for wanting you to touch me again." My statement came out flat and hard.

His cheeks darkened. He looked away. "You are in the Burn. It's a common feeling."

"I deal with the Burn every day. I know it backwards and forwards, and how it affects me, and how to appease it, increase

78

it, play to it. Feed or starve it. I've tried all tactics. I know how it curls in my veins and makes my skin flame. The sexual arousal from it runs through my body. It's wonderful, actually. Most of the time. At worst, it's an inconvenience. It doesn't make me feel lonely, only pent up. But you, you came into my mind. And now, now I can't think of anything else."

"That's—that's—you don't know what you're saying."

"All right, then. Maybe I don't. But you can't deny that something else might be there. For us. Between us?"

His brow furrowed. His desk chair squeaked. "That's not even a possibility."

"It is. You're unbonded. I feel that. I smell it. I surge with it. But there's something more. Don't you feel it?"

He started to shake his head.

Before he could cut me off, I said, "They say bonded mates will break down walls to get to each other during the Alpha's Burn. I don't know what you feel regarding me and my Burn. But at your next Burn, I think I will feel it." I was being overly bold now, in all new territory. I spoke from my inner emotions, nothing to do with rational thinking. But to my heart, everything I said was true. "It's because you touched me. It's forbidden for a reason. The gloves are there for a reason. I didn't really believe it until now. Until you touched me. But it made me happy, too, so I don't think it's wrong."

His face flushed. He looked angry or—no—that wasn't anger. He was mortified. Afraid.

"I have no clue what your Burn will do to me, how it will affect me," I continued. "That's why I said I think I'm dying. Because I want you too much."

Geo got up from his chair so rapidly it rocked back and forth. He would not look at me.

"I do know what I'm feeling, don't you. What if--" I prodded.

"You are fine." He interrupted. "You'll be fine."

I stood. "If you're sure, then." I let my voice trail. "I can't help but wonder. And if you are wrong, what will happen to me?"

"Nothing. You're fine, believe me." His head was lowered, his fists tight at his sides. "You'll continue with the freedoms I've given you. You will be treated fairly and I will make sure you're safe. I'll have a meeting with the doctors to discuss a possible field trip for the future. As I said, one step at a time."

"But Geo. You must know."

"What?" He sounded slightly impatient.

"I'm not safe. I'm not safe anymore. From you."

His head swiveled upward. His eyes locked onto me. We stared for several seconds, unmoving. His gaze was fierce and strong and pained all at the same time.

"You need to leave now," he said through gritted teeth.

"I'm not safe," I repeated. "From your Burn. We'll find out, won't we?"

He shook his head. It was a dismissal. Already he was turning away from me.

"You know I'm right. No matter what, there is something between us."

But he wouldn't acknowledge me. He wouldn't respond.

Only my third meeting with the king, the man I wanted to mate-bond me, and I'd blown it.

Chapter Eight

Geo

I stood before Doctor Prim with my white sleeve rolled up to the elbow as he fastened the tourniquet.

"This is to be kept private," I said.

"All matters between a doctor and patient are private, sir," he replied.

"How long before the test is complete?"

"Two days."

He drew two vials of blood in a matter of seconds. Then he released the tourniquet and pressed a bandage over the small wound.

The lights hurt my eyes. I couldn't wait to get out of there, go home and take a long hot shower.

Misha. He was all I could think of. He'd said he felt a bond between us. While I, too, could not get him out of my mind, I denied it. He couldn't be right. He couldn't.

I'd touched him, but that was all. Could a bond form from just that?

With Sylphs, so little was still known, especially about ones Misha's age. Adult and sane and with properties none had had a chance to study before, there was nothing to go on but his words, experiences, everything like new. He should have been a lab rat. Instead, he had been stuffed away here at Riverside Colony and long forgotten.

It shouldn't have happened.

I should not have touched him.

*

The night after my conversation with Misha, I drove home without really seeing. I don't know how I made it through the streets unscathed.

When I collapsed on my couch with a sandwich and turned on the TV, I forced myself to relax. It was difficult, but my own surroundings helped. The drone of a sitcom. The sound of an occasional car driving down the lane outside. My familiar things: books, pictures, blankets all made my version of a nest.

I'd lived here seven years. I'd been content. I didn't feel I was missing out on anything like an Omega partner or a family. I was still young. I had plenty of time for thoughts about that in the future.

Still, Misha's blunt words this afternoon had sent a shock through my system.

It was true. I'd had fantasies of him day and night since bathing him in the tub at the colony, but I put them off to my own vulnerabilities within the Sylph allure. Nothing more.

For him to insinuate it was more rattled my very being. That was why I'd gone for the blood test. If it came back negative, I could show him he was wrong. I would have facts and science to back me up. No matter how much I wanted him, he needed to know there was nothing between us. That he would not feel the call of my Alpha Burn mixing with his own. That he was safe.

But his own Burn. I could almost feel it right now. It teased me. Taunted me. But no, it had to be only my imagination.

What if he was right?

I picked up my phone and tapped up my calendar, checking and double checking the date of my next Burn.

My skin felt hot and my cock was erect. But no, I wasn't due to Burn for another three weeks.

Various things might throw an Alpha off of his Burn schedule. The pregnancy of his Omega. Death of his Omega. Drugs. Head injury. Illness. Very old age.

I had none of those problems.

But I *had* taken a job where I had let myself visit with and touch a Sylph. With my bare hands. There was a reason regulations, such as glove-wearing, were in place. There were reasons only bonded Alphas and Omegas worked in Sylph institutions.

I should never have accepted the position. My half-bond with Mase was obviously gone. It didn't protect me. Despite my long-buried grief, it was as if it had never been.

I stared at the TV for a long time, willing myself not to think at all. Now and again, I picked up my phone and scrolled through messages from friends. I answered none of them.

None of my friends were close enough to confide in.

I was truly alone.

*

I read the words on the paper Doctor Prim handed me three times before I folded it up and put it in my blazer pocket.

"There is no mistake," he said.

He stared at me a little long for my comfort. His eyes were dark and unreadable, but I knew he wanted to ask me questions. The answers to which were none of his business. Not really.

Except for the fact that any answers I might give irrevocably involved the proper running of the Sylph colony. Answers which I could never reveal to another soul.

It had been two long days waiting for the results of my blood test. I'd worked on auto-pilot. I'd avoided the staff.

Tory was the only person I spoke to, and he came across as far too forward. He asked too many questions. I kept my office door closed between us hoping to deter him because a lot of his work involved the work I was doing for Misha.

I simply wanted to put everything on hold.

I had not visited Misha since his visit to me in my office. And he had not come by again to request my attention.

But every thought I had was of him and that got worse with each new day. I was burning, burning and it wouldn't stop. It wasn't out of control, and it wasn't like a real Burn. But I was hot all the time. I'd masturbated more in the past few days than I had in the past two years outside of a Burn.

My test results told me why.

At my desk, I took the folded piece of paper out of my jacket pocket and set it in front of me. I didn't need to look at the words again. I'd read it three times. They were clear. There was no mistake. So said Doctor Prim.

I had a two point nine rated bond with Misha, and it was a very solid beginning of something that simply could not be. We hadn't had sex. I hadn't knotted. We were never together. But two point nine was high out of an over all perfect rating of ten. That rating was something that started usually when two people were sleeping together and found themselves becoming compatible. We hadn't done any of that. It was taboo to sleep with a Sylph, and I never had, but who would believe me? If word got out, I'd be fired, possibly arrested. Yet I'd never bedded him. Never.

I had no one to talk to about this. There were no textbooks on this subject. Nothing. I was alone.

And so was Misha.

Our lives were in danger, him from me, and mine from the law. I had no solutions. But I'd have to come up with one soon to protect us both.

Chapter Nine

Misha

The day seemed very blue from dawn until dusk. It lasted a thousand years. At least to my perception.

King Geo continued to avoid me. I continued to Burn for him and only him.

I knew why. There was something between us. I wasn't Omega, so it couldn't be an Alpha/Omega bond, but it was something strong. Something unavoidable. Why didn't he come to me?

What I felt was about more than sex. He didn't have to worry I would attack him. I'd proven it to him by my mature behavior in his office.

Still, I was stupid to think he would come. I got caught up in fantasy very easily. It was both my flaw and my strength. Fantasy had saved my sanity.

But this particular desire I had, this fantasy of wanting more with Geo was impossible. To have any sort of connection that led to more? I could tell he would never allow it. He had a life outside. I was trapped here forever and I knew it. Nothing could come of this. Only suffering.

The worst was, the more I tried to block him from my mind, the more I burned. I was being a ridiculous child. An insane Sylph no different from Cedric.

I had proven nothing to Geo. That was why he didn't visit.

I stopped walking the two floors I was allowed on. I stopped going out for exercise. I stopped everything. I slept late and ate little. Sometimes I watched my TV, but I didn't really pay attention to the shows. I didn't speak to my guards or the nurses at all.

I lived like a captive.

Four days went by.

The fifth morning a knock came at my door. I was sitting up, having only just awakened.

"Come in."

Geo's assistant entered. Tory. The one who smelled different from all the others, more acrid. The one who looked at me funny when I visited Geo's office.

For a moment, he stood on the threshold to my room, large and dark. He made the air turn thin. I couldn't get enough breath just to look at him.

I loved everyone I met, but this one made me nervous.

"There have been reports funneling in about you."

I waited to see if he would say more. Like hello. Or, how are you feeling?

"What's wrong with you?" he asked.

"I am very well, thank you." I was not about to discuss anything with this Alpha who wasn't a nurse or a doctor, and who had nothing to do with me.

"I'm here to tell you he doesn't want anything to do with you. So if not eating and exercising is some way to get his attention, then stop. It won't work."

Who was he talking about? Geo? How could he know?

I rose from the bed. I wore nothing and his eyes widened, taking on a strange sheen.

"There are reports about me. Funneled to you?" I came closer and he looked as if he wanted to back away, but he held his ground.

I liked that he seemed scared. Or angry. I liked that I appeared to have power over him.

I wasn't erect because I'd already taken care of that before he knocked, but I was hot all over, quivering, flushed. The skin at my temples cooled in the air from my sweat. My hair was pushed over one eye and I brushed it back with a graceful gesture. I knew I was beautiful, even still half-asleep. Maybe more so. I was a Sylph. So be it.

Tory licked his lips. His scent went hot with a smell like the blacktop where I exercised when it got over-heated in the summertime. Like before, I smelled a bond within him, but faint. What had happened to this man?

Tory shut the door behind him. He looked me slowly up and down. His pants grew tighter at the crotch.

I took a deep breath. The people who worked here did not normally behave this way. They came in twos. Or they kept my door open when dealing with me so the guards were within hearing distance. Even Geo had kept to that obvious protocol.

Where were my guards?

"I know you're trying to get his attention," Tory said. "Even now, you're trying to seduce me with your bare body and your faked innocence. You know exactly what you're doing. And you're doing the same thing with Geo, aren't you?"

Ah, so he didn't know for sure what was between me and Geo.

Slowly, I reached for my robe. In that moment, Tory dashed forward and grabbed my hand. He was gloved, but it didn't seem to matter. He pulled my body to him hard, wrenching one of my arms up behind my back.

I was no weakling. I'd worked hard to keep myself in shape from the exercise I'd been allowed. I elbowed him in the ribs and twisted out of his hold though he still had a strong grip on my arm. It hurt, but panic fueled me. No one had ever attacked me here before. No one dared.

I cried out. A pounding began from outside. Not Tracy's usual thumps. Not Cedric. But at my door. My guards.

That was when I realized Tory had flipped the door lock from the outside before coming in. They had keys, but after Geo had given me freedom in the castle, they no longer were used to using them for my door.

I heard a scramble outside, and a jingling.

Tory heard it, too.

He pulled me close again, even as I shoved against his chest, and he ran his hands down the sides of my body.

"So soft and hard at the same time." His fingers traced my ribs, my waist, and my stomach before finding my cock. He wrapped them around it, still gloved, and pulled hard.

White pain shot through me and into my vision. I cried out, a yell that made Cedric start screaming from his own room. "Misha," he called. "Misha!"

I scrambled with my hands, my nails clawing at his sleeves, grabbing, pinching.

I kept thinking the door to my room would open, the guards would rush in and this terrible thing would stop happening. But something was wrong. They were taking too long.

"Stop! Stop!" I yelled. I didn't want to feel this way. I didn't want to fight. I'd never had a violent thought in my life. But I didn't want this. I didn't want Tory.

The sudden realization stopped me.

I wanted everyone. I loved everyone. I wished for the touches of anyone who crossed my path. Why not this Alpha?

I should love him but all I felt was contempt and fear. He had that bitter odor. His touch hurt. His gloved touch. Strange. I felt no arousal at all from it.

In that moment when I'd stopped fighting, he leaned into me. His free hand came to my throat and grasped it, closing tight. He had big hands and he closed his fingers around the sides of my neck pressing hard. He knew where my windpipe was and the heel of his hand pushed until I gasped.

I opened my mouth, struggling for air. My hands were trapped between us. I stopped fighting at once. It would get me nowhere. I was strong, but Tory was stronger.

All I could do was lean into him as he pressed against me, allowing my air to become totally blocked. I let my muscles relax until I felt him relax.

Little sparkles began to form around the edges of my vision.

It was now or never.

With a sudden lurch, I bent into his hand on my neck hoping he wouldn't actually break anything, and managed to brush my face up against his shoulder. My open mouth found cloth only, but I gambled on more. I bit down and my teeth grazed muscle. I pushed harder, my mind spinning now from lack of air, and bit down again as hard as I could.

I heard a howl. It seemed to come up from the bowels of the building.

Tory's grip on my throat lessened and I was able to back up, my teeth ripping cloth and flesh as I went.

As if from out of nowhere, something struck me across the head.

The world went black.

Chapter Ten

Geo

My cell phone sang on the edge of my desk.

Glancing down, I saw it was one of the nurses on the second floor.

I hit *answer*.

At first, all I could hear was a lot of background noise, and something that sounded like a scuffle. There was a rumble of murmuring voices, then a shout.

I spoke into the phone. "Geo, here. What's going on?"

"He's gone rogue, I think," said a voice. I didn't recognize who it was.

A loud knock at my door made me look up. Whoever it was didn't wait for my response. Instead, my office door swung wide open banging against the wall to reveal a guard.

"What the--?"

The guard said, "It's Misha."

"What?"

I jumped up and ran out the door, following the guard to the elevators.

As we jogged, I said, "What's going on?"

"Misha and Tory. They're both injured."

"What?" But I realized as I'd run into the hallway, Tory was not at his desk.

The guard pushed the button for the elevator. As we waited, I noted he was breathing hard, his cheeks dark. He'd run all the way to my office.

"Tell me."

"We don't know. Just that they're hurt. They're both being brought to the hospital wing."

Just then the elevator doors opened. Inside were the two on-shift doctors, one of whom was Prim, surrounding a gurney. On the gurney, naked and unconscious, lay Misha. *My Misha.*

I don't know why I thought of him that way, but it was an instant response. I couldn't hold back. My heart jammed into my throat.

I shoved my way through the circle of doctors and nurses. I saw red and purple bruising around his throat, and scratches down the right side of his ribs. He had an intubation tube down his throat and a nurse compressed air steadily into it.

"Out of the way!" yelled Prim.

"Is he alive?" I asked.

Prim glanced up at me. "He is. But we have to get him to the ICU at once."

"Let's go!" Prim yelled at the group.

People ran. The gurney was pushed at a speed I had to jog to keep up with.

Once in the hospital, he was taken down a long hall to a fully equipped intensive care room. Everyone talked at once as I followed.

Once inside the room, an I.V. was strapped to Misha's hand. I saw that his other arm also looked bruised, perhaps broken. His face was so pale. He lay still. Far too still.

I turned to the guard who'd run into my office and who'd been following us the entire way. "I want a report. Right now!"

"I only know the emergency beacon on my phone went off for the second floor. I was there, but in another corridor. I came running."

"What happened?"

"I saw the guards breaking into the door of Misha's room. I don't know why they didn't use their key. I heard sounds of yelling and rushed to the door. When I got there, I saw Misha on the floor and the guards were fighting."

"Fighting? With whom?"

"Tory. He was half-crazed, sir. There was blood all over his throat. He kept pushing and shoving at the guards. He knocked one against the wall. Another grabbed him from behind and he slammed him to the floor nearly on top of Misha. It was like he had super strength. More guards had come before me, and managed to get the cuffs on him, but he wouldn't stop struggling. Someone said to call the doctors. Someone else told me to run to your office and get you."

"Where is Tory?"

"They had to sedate him. He's being brought here, too."

I glanced at Misha and could tell that everything that could be was being done for him, then walked to the door to look up and down the hall. Then I saw them. Another group and another gurney coming through the hospital doors. Several guards followed, limping. Another guard was being supported by a nurse.

As one limping guard passed by me, I recognized him immediately. One of Misha's day guards. Laro.

"Laro, what happened?"

"Tory locked himself in Misha's room. He—he went berserk. He said he had come by on a well-check authorized by you. But he—he—I don't know what happened with him, sir."

When I looked at Tory being rolled by, certainly he was injured. There was blood at his collar and his white shirt was torn, some of the buttons missing at the top. He looked asleep. But he was breathing.

I had an instinctive response to jump on the gurney, wrap my hands around his throat and shake him awake. Demand to know why he'd gone to Misha's room, why he'd lied to the guards, and why my Misha was now on a respirator fighting for his life. I had the urge to claw at him, rip and tear until he submitted, until he gave way and whimpered back to whatever hovel he'd come from.

He'd worked here for ten years. There hadn't been anything in his performance record I could see that made him unstable. I certainly hadn't warmed to him, and he was wary of

92

me as well, but I had brushed that off as me being the new chief of staff. It always took time to earn the trust of one's staff at a new place.

My hands clenched to fists as I held back from wanting to pummel him into a puddle of blood and bone. Never had I felt this sort of violence in me.

I reeled from the onslaught of nearly uncontrollable emotion and forced myself to turn away and rush back to Misha's side.

I stood at the foot of the bed. Nurses milled about his side. Doctor Prim was gently manipulating Misha's injured arm. The remaining doctor had gone to look at Tory in the next cubicle.

"Give me an update," I ordered.

Prim said, "His windpipe is intact. But the swelling around it means we have to keep him on the respirator. I can't tell yet how he'll come out of this. How long he was deprived of oxygen, and how strong his constitution is will be the deciding factors."

"Will there be brain damage?"

"He has brain activity in the normal range, but as I said, we can't know for certain until he wakes up."

I came around the nurse on the other side of the bed and looked down at my beautiful Misha. Someone had covered his body with a sheet up to his waist. His arm lay at his side, a tube inserted on the outside of his hand just above the wrist. I slid my palm underneath his hand and held it.

The nurse glanced at me but said nothing. I wasn't in protocol. Again. I wasn't using gloves. Again. But I didn't care. Not now. I wanted to feel his skin, his heat, his pulse. I wanted to assure myself that he was still alive.

His skin was cool, his fingers actually cold as I wove mine with his. I placed my other hand over the top of his, ignoring the I.V.

Another nurse came around my other side, nudging me. Irritated, I turned to see him fiddling with the bed straps.

"What are you doing?" I asked.

He looked wide-eyed for a moment. "Protocol. And doctor's orders, sir. Whenever a patient attacks a member of staff, they are to be treated as dangerous and subdued according to safety regulations. Even in ICU."

Prim nodded, validating the nurse's words.

"He's the least violent patient in the ward," I said. "In the entire colony. It was Misha who was attacked!"

"Until the reports are filed and a proper investigation is conducted, those are the rules," Prim said.

"But it's Tory who should be strapped down. Locked away, in fact!"

"You can, of course, lead the investigation and make your reports as to your findings and recommendations in the appropriate manner," Prim added.

As the nurse fastened the soft restraint about Misha's wrist, I never let go of his hand. Prim ordered a wrist-splint on his other arm. "It's only a sprain," he assured me. But the bruising on his fine, smooth skin was like a thundercloud.

After the nurse fastened the wrist-guard, he loosely secured the second restraint. He then moved down to Misha's ankles, lifting the sheet and securing them as well.

It infuriated me. I had to force my breathing to remain steady.

For the next hour, I refused to leave Misha's side. I used my cell to relay orders to my staff as I began to organize my investigation.

All the while, I continued to stroke Misha's arm. I talked to him, telling him he was all right, that he was safe. Over and over again, much to the surprise of the nurses, I spoke to him softly. I kept my vigil.

At the end of the second hour into this terrible drama, I heard low moans coming from outside Misha's cubicle. Then a few shouts. I recognized the voice.

Tory was waking up.

I hated to leave Misha. But I wanted to confront Tory. I wasn't sure I'd be able to control myself. I wasn't sure I wanted to.

I looked up at the nurse who was continually monitoring his readouts. "Come get me if there is any change. I'll be in the next room."

"Yes, sir."

When I came around to the doorway of Tory's cubicle I saw he was, like Misha, restrained.

The Alpha who had been my wary assistant tugged angrily at the cuffs on his wrists. His dark hair was slicked back from his head, and his face was flushed. In a hoarse voice, he yelled, "Let me loose! You can't do this! I have rights!"

His shirt had been cut off and his bare chest rose and fell with his breaths. A white bandage sealed over his wound, extending from his inner shoulder toward his neck. It wasn't large, but there were still light traces of blood on his skin around the bandaged area.

Tory tossed his head back and forth on the pillow, his mouth a grimace. He actually growled.

Without bothering to try to talk to him, I went to Doctor Prim's office.

Prim looked up as he entered.

"What is wrong with Tory? Why is he behaving like this?"

"I've ordered another sedation and am currently running blood tests."

"Well, I certainly can't interview him in his current state. Have you contacted his Omega?"

"I can't get hold of him. Tory's files say he is bonded to a man named Lix. There's a cell number. I've tried it several times. No answer."

"Do you know if anyone around here knows Tory? Or is friends with him? Or socializes with him outside of work?"

The doctor shook his head.

"How was he injured?"

"It appears to be a bite."

"Misha bit him?"

"That is what is indicated. It's not life threatening. A surface abrasion, but it bled a lot."

"I know in my heart Misha didn't just attack him. Something is very wrong with Tory."

"It appears that way to me, too. We'll find out when the labs come back."

"I don't want to leave Misha's side, but I need to begin the interviews. And of course, now I have no assistant."

Prim frowned at me. "If you need to leave, you can be assured I will look after him."

"I know. But I--" My body and mind wanted to go back to Misha right now. The urge was so strong to be with him, to sit at his side, to touch him. But why?

But of course. The blood test. The bond.

I knew Prim wanted to ask me why I took such an interest in one patient. Why I wouldn't leave. But he was polite enough to keep his questions to himself.

When I walked back to Misha's cubicle, Tory's yells had quieted. The sedation was working. But how long would they have to keep him that way? If he didn't improve, he'd need to be transported to a real Alpha hospital where they dealt with dangerous Alphas.

Misha lay as I'd left him, unmoving, pale in the face, the bruising about his neck darkening to violent shades of purple and red.

I came to his side again. Behind me, I heard a shuffle against the floor. I looked over my shoulder to see the nurse bring a chair around so I could sit.

"Thank you." I was worn out from everything, though I felt like I'd done nothing at all.

The past few days I had been working hard, trying not to think about Misha. I thought if I could break my cycle of fantasizing about him and thinking I needed him everything would be okay. I thought if I avoided everything, even my own

96

symptoms, I would not feel like I was entering the Alpha Burn early. I could deny everything and break the bond, the way I had done with Mase. Only that hadn't worked very well, had it?

Why did I think this partial bond would be any different?

Now I wondered, if I had not ignored Misha, would this disaster have been averted?

I stared at his quiet, pale face and held his hand. Everything he was going through felt like fractures in my heart. He was inside me. I couldn't doubt it now. I didn't need a positive blood test result to prove it.

Doctor Prim came back to check on him some time later. Prim looked at Misha, then up at the screens with their read-outs.

"I've given him medication to reduce the swelling. So far, so good. He's stable. Give it a night. He should be more improved by tomorrow."

My chest ached. My muscles hurt. Everything was pain. I touched Misha and that was what was in my mind, what I felt.

"Is he in pain?"

Prim shook his head no. "We're keeping him sedated while he's on the respirator. He isn't aware. Even if you see him move around, he won't remember it when he finally wakes."

"But I can't stand to think he's suffering right now." I rubbed at the sharp edge of pain in the middle of my chest.

"He's fine for now. He's in a gray state where, even when he's not asleep, he's still in an alpha-state."

"Will he feel the Burn?"

"No. This extreme sedation will upset that routine. He won't feel it. But I can't keep it up for long. His body won't take it."

Even Alphas sometimes used sedatives for a temporary relief of the Burn, but it didn't work long-term and the side effects could be bad. The worst effect was when the drug wore off the Burn would return, sometimes worse than ever. It could cause out of control behavior and that was why Alphas who used such drugs needed to be monitored by physicians at all times.

"For the night, he will rest. He won't remember any of this, I assure you," Prim said. "You should go home soon. Get some rest yourself."

I took a deep breath.

I nodded but didn't answer.

I still had so much work to do. I would bring charges against Tory. I would make him pay for what he'd done to Misha.

Prim sighed. "I'll have a nurse bring some dinner by for you."

"Thank you."

There was no way I was leaving Misha's side. Let the rumors begin. Let them all talk.

My Misha.

I would never abandon him.

Chapter Eleven

Misha

Everything around me swirled in a sea of gray punctured by strange green lights. Something was choking me.

I tried to cough but that didn't work. I choked again, gagging.

A voice in the murkiness said, "Cough again."

I obeyed and the obstacle in my throat came loose. It was long and hard and it came out in a single slipping motion after which I gasped on my own. Air filled my dry mouth. I moaned but the sound that came out was more of a whispered crackle.

My vision slowly returned, though blurred. I kept blinking away tears as I coughed again and again, my throat itching and dry.

"Water." The word I tried to speak sounded like a croak.

I saw motion, two figures all in shades of gray and white. The only color I could see so far were green lights blinking off to my right. Light overhead hurt my eyes.

The motion of an arm came close to my face and I drew back.

Someone stuck a straw between my lips. I instantly sucked and cool water filled my mouth. I swallowed slowly, savoring the liquid on my dry throat, and the hint of cold.

Thoughts in my mind seemed to sweep in all at once as I tried to find a context for where I was and why I felt so terrible. What had happened? My throat ached. And my wrist. Had I been injured?

My arms were at my sides and I moved them as I tried to sit up, but something tugged at my wrists, keeping them in place. I felt another stiff sleeve on my right wrist, the one that hurt. When I tried to bend my knees, the same sort of stricture held my feet in place at my ankles.

The straw slipped from my mouth and a voice said, "Lie still if you can. You're safe."

I knew that voice. I'd know it anywhere—in my dreams, in my deepest thoughts, in my fantasies and my nightmares. Geo.

I whispered his name.

He said, "Right here. I'm right here."

Fingers touched the top of my hand. Ungloved. The tips glided across my skin sending tendrils of shimmering, tickly feelings up my arm.

I'd been cold as I had wakened. Now I was warm.

Geo knew better than to touch me. This was on purpose. What could it mean?

My throat ached fiercely. My muscles tightened with the pain as I grew more and more aware. I lifted my hips and groaned.

"He's hurting," Geo said.

"I've given him something for it," said another voice.

I blinked up at Geo, willing him into focus. After a moment, there he was, magnificent, glowing, the visiting king who showed compassion, who took an interest in me until he was scared away by my strangeness, my alien culture.

But what had happened? Where were we? Certainly, we were still in the castle at the edge of the green sea where mad princes were held in chambers away from the world of Alpha and Omega men. At least, it was a comfort to think so.

Slowly, the memories began to seep in.

I remembered Tory coming into my room and shutting the door. He touched me and there was agony. And then nothing. I remembered thinking I was dying and in that moment the thumps and screams of my brothers went silent. Everything stopped. The world went away.

Geo stroked the top of my forearm.

My body heated up fast, the Burn overtaking me. I tried to lift my hands but straps held them down.

"Where am I?" I mouthed the words as they passed through my throat like air.

"You're in the colony hospital. You're fine. Don't worry."

I turned my head to glance at the straps holding me.

"For your own safety. We didn't want you pulling out the I.V. or respirator."

I wasn't sure I believed him. After what happened, I was sure we would be taking backward steps. My room would be locked again. My freedoms curtailed.

Geo bent closer to me. I could feel his body heat and smell his cologne—or maybe it was just him. Coffee, which I'd only ever had once and liked, and hand sanitizer, but also deeper beneath all that a bouquet of salt and tart and flame, savory. I wanted him with my body. My mouth. My eyes. My mind.

"Do you remember what happened?

I gave a little shrug.

"Tory is injured."

My eyes widened.

"You bit him."

"I don't remember." My voice garbled the words but he understood me.

How could I have bitten him? I would never hurt anyone. I didn't remember biting, but I did remember him hurting me. Had I lashed out at the last minute? If so, I did it on pure instinct, and with no intent to harm.

I frowned, trying to remember. Slowly, slices of memory, faint and disturbing, came back to me. His hand around my neck so tight I couldn't breathe. My own hands trapped between us, trying to rise to his shoulders. Trying to push him back. Later, grabbing, pulling. My head moving into his deadly squeeze. My nose briefly touching his shirt. I'd opened my mouth. I'd caught my teeth against the cloth and closed down hard.

Tory had been about to kill me. I knew why. I remembered that part.

He was burning when he came into my room, but not from the Burn. His response was for me. Just for me.

Geo felt similar to me, but smelled sweeter. And his gestures were non-threatening. Controlled.

Tory had been out of control.

I wanted to tell Geo all of this. But I didn't have the energy yet. Or the voice.

My body ached but something in my system dulled the discomfort. I was grateful for the drug, though it did nothing to calm my erection.

I squirmed to make myself more comfortable.

Geo adjusted my blanket, his eyes lingering at my midsection for a moment. His cheeks pinked a little. I loved his response.

At that moment, a doctor came into my room.

As my mind spun on the drug, the doctor and Geo spoke to each other.

"He's doing very well. A dramatic improvement. I'll keep him for a couple of days, though," said the doctor.

"I'm very glad to hear it." Geo's hand had fallen away from my arm and rested on the side of my bed.

"He'll be murky for awhile. I've prescribed something for the pain. Hopefully, he'll mostly sleep."

"Good."

The doctor turned away from me, hand blocking his mouth. But I still heard him.

"Tory will not talk. To anyone."

I watched Geo nod. "I'll try to talk to him again later."

"He'll be transferred to Carson later this afternoon. We can't keep him here. There's no point. They have a great psychiatric facility there." He paused. "I've already made my report. The authorities will intervene. He'll probably go for a three day observation. From there, they may or may not press charges."

102

"*I'll* press charges," Geo said.

"Is that wise? What would that say to the staff about you? Sylphs are unpredictable. Accidents happen."

"This was no accident. Misha is harmless. This was an Alpha out of control. He's not in the Burn so something happened with him in his mind or his body—I don't know. But he didn't talk to anyone. He didn't ask for time off. Nothing."

As they spoke about me and about Tory, my mind went into a fog. The voices drifted over me, making me feel left out and lonelier than ever. I'd always felt safe here at the colony, at the castle.

But then Geo came. And everything had changed.

Later, I was allowed to get up and use the facilities. A nurse, gloved and covered head to toe, everything but the eyes, disconnected my I.V. and took off the restraints. He helped me shower with a guard standing just inside the bathroom as well.

I wanted an orgasm badly, more than anything at that moment, but I held myself back from touching myself. I could control it. I had a rational mind. A clear mind. I wasn't like the others, I told myself. Or maybe I was just like them and had deluded myself this whole time.

What I really wanted—*who* I really wanted was Geo. My longing for him surged through my body. I wanted to laugh and cry at the same time.

The nurse helped me dry off and wrapped me in a soft, pale blue robe.

When I re-entered the hospital room, Geo was sitting in a chair by the window tapping on his tablet. He looked up as the nurse helped me back into my bed and re-fastened the straps about my wrists.

"Leave his legs free for now," Geo said. His green eyes flashed.

"I'm not a danger, I assure you," I said.

The nurse said nothing, but I could see he didn't believe it. He left.

My beloved Geo got up and adjusted the wrist straps a little looser. "I'm sorry this happened to you."

"I'm sorry, too," I said. My voice was raspy, but the words were no longer garbled.

"Are you comfortable? Are you in pain?"

The medication had helped me, but I still felt discomfort, especially when I turned my head and the pressure of the bruising on my neck sent sharp twinges into my jaw, head and shoulders. But it was manageable.

"I'm comfortable," I replied.

"I wish there was more I could do."

I raised my hand as if to reach out to him. He did not reach back.

"You touched me and I feel it still," I whispered. "That's what you are doing for me. Even now. And it's wonderful."

His beautiful face darkened. The light in the room seemed brighter for a moment. Hurting my eyes. His presence, still and unmoving at my side, went into me like a swirl of air, and his scent—I couldn't get enough!

"I apologize. That is gross misconduct on my part."

"Even if it is, you keep doing it. I felt your hand on mine. And though I was sleeping, a part of me knows you were here all night."

He nodded, eyebrows coming together but not as a frown, more like confusion. "I was very worried."

"I know." I couldn't help it, the response popped from my mouth even though I was still unsure.

He swallowed. "We can't talk like this. We should never talk like this."

"Why?"

"There is a chain of protocols in place for a reason."

"I know. This isn't about protocols. This is something different."

He turned his head and looked across the bed at the wall by the door. "It isn't."

"It is," I argued. "I've never felt like I do now. Like something is missing. It isn't about the Sylph Burn. It isn't about anything except--" I stopped, swallowed hard. "Except you. I can't stop seeing images of you in my mind, and it makes me think I'm losing my mind. But I'm sane. You know this. And so are you."

He said nothing.

"What has happened?"

"No matter what it is," he said in a monotone, "it's wrong. It's taboo. It's against the rules and against Alpha law."

I knew this, but I didn't want to know it. "Oh."

It was confirmed then. I was a burden. A problem. Something broken that could never be fixed.

I heard it in his voice. Felt it in my mind. Geo didn't want me. Couldn't want me. Any other path would lead to his downfall.

My eyes stung. I held my breath. Nothing would ever change for me. I never thought it would. So why this reaction? Why not fight harder? But not if it meant Geo would suffer. My life was trapped. It couldn't be over because it had never begun. And never would.

How could I miss something I'd never had?

It was apparent something inside me had changed. Tory had seen it and the result was an attack upon me. Geo saw it and felt it because we were connected. It meant I wasn't safe. It also meant my freedoms needed to be curtailed again. I'd be like Cedric and Tracy, locked away. Eventually, maybe I, too, would go mad.

"I'm sorry, Misha," Geo said. "None of this should ever have happened to you."

I wanted to fight his words, but I couldn't. I felt them weave into me, his feelings, his despair. I shared it. We were on the same wavelength.

The room became a blur. The ceiling light glared too white. The monitors with their soft hums were too loud. Everything around me became exaggerated in one giant irritation. My wet hair on my pillow felt cold and alien. Even the sheets against my skin hurt.

"I'm sorry," Geo said again.

"Just go," I said, hearing my voice as if from another realm.

After a minute, I heard the soft rustle of his clothing as he stood. I heard his footfalls across the hard, tile floor. The door opened and closed.

He'd left me. He'd left me alone.

Chapter Twelve

Geo

"I'd like to see you about Tory's report." Once again, I stood in the doorway of Doctor Prim's office.

"Come in." He waved his hand toward me.

Prim was older than I by about thirty years, but it didn't show. He looked young and healthy, an Alpha man in his prime.

I'd read his resume, as I had all of the staff when I took the job. He'd been bonded for twenty years. He had three children from one litter, which was not uncommon. His kids included two Alphas and an Omega, and he and his bondmate were raising them all, unlike some couples who sent their Omegas off to be brought up and educated on chattel farms, considered to be an acceptable option for Omega children. While the Omegas had few rights and very little say in their futures, like my own childhood friend Mase, many families chose to keep those children and love them. The world wasn't entirely crazy and emotionless.

When I sat across from Prim, he began.

"The report on Tory is muddled, but we do know his Omega is not living at his address. We're still trying to locate him."

I crossed my arms and pressed my back into the leather of the chair. "If his Omega left him, protocols dictate Tory should have reported it. If his bond is in jeopardy, or worse broken, it is a violation of his work contract."

"Which is probably the very reason he didn't report it. He didn't want to lose his job," Prim said.

"But I wouldn't have fired him outright. I would've made sure he worked isolated from patients, including Misha who I would have banned from my office."

"You know better." Prim sighed. "You would have laid him off. It's board policy. You would have banned Tory from the colony. It has nothing to do with Misha being able to walk the halls or not."

"I'm still new here. We don't know each other. But if it came to laying off Tory, I would have helped Tory find new work. I would have given him a good letter of recommendation."

"He didn't know that." Prim put his elbows on his desk and clasped his hands in front of him. "At any rate, he's being transferred and that will be on record. His job is lost. You'll need a new assistant."

I couldn't help but think Prim was being a bit cold. He'd worked here as long as Tory. He knew the man even if they weren't friends.

If he knew anything at all about what was going on—which was nothing, really, it had to be nothing—between me and Misha, I'd be out as well. For some reason, the thought did not panic me. I knew I could do this job and do it well, but I wasn't in love with it. My biggest fear was being arrested. It would end my career. I would have to start over from scratch with, technically, a criminal record.

Prim continued to talk but I heard very little, until he said, "By the way, I never congratulated you on your newly forming bond."

My skin flamed beneath my shirt and trousers. I know my face had to show my shock. "Yes, thank you. I think maybe it happened at a chattel farm I last visited. The Omega and I got along quite well. We were extremely compatible."

"Excellent. Well, good then. We don't have to worry. Your job should have gone to a mated Alpha and now it looks like that qualification will be soon satisfied. Are you dating? Have you proposed yet?"

"Uh. No. Not yet."

My body wanted to shiver and melt at the same time. This couldn't be happening. I couldn't be bonded. I hadn't formed a bond with my last Omega partner, and I had never had sex with Misha.

"Can that test be run again? I just want to be sure."

"There is little margin for error," Prim replied, frowning.

"Please? I'm not feeling what I think I should be feeling. Run it again."

"Do you want a new test on new blood?"

"Yes."

Later, after the vial of my blood was packaged and sent to a nearby lab the colony always used, I passed by Misha's room. Even though our last parting had felt somewhat final, and I'd promised myself I'd stay away from him, I couldn't resist going in one more time. I risked everything by doing so, but my emotions over-ruled my rational mind. I had to see him. It hurt me internally to stay away from him.

I didn't think about any consequences, or what I might do. I existed only in the now. Today was all.

As I came to his side and sat, the tension in my body almost immediately released. My heart-rate calmed. But my mind wasn't working right and I knew it.

Prim had brought up the blood test and there was just no denial of it. It was fresh on my mind again. Clear as day. I was forming a bond with Misha and it should have been impossible. Skin to skin contact should not have been sufficient to cause a two point nine rating. We had not shared bodily fluids. We hadn't even kissed.

Misha slept, his long lashes brushing the tops of his cheeks, his breathing slow and peaceful. My chest felt filled with buffeting air. My Misha. I couldn't stop thinking of him that way.

The blanket covered him to the sternum. His bare chest gently rose and fell, hairless and perfect, the pecs well-defined, the nipples the loveliest shade of pink I'd ever seen, perfect and round, perky and pointed. I wanted to brush my fingertips over them, feel the taut and heated skin.

The bruising on his neck remained a violent thunderstorm of color, of wounding.

My muscles clenched. I thought of Tory and wanted to kill. I'd never had that sort of instinct in my life. But I knew if Tory crossed my path right now, I might not be able to control myself. He'd hurt my Misha. My mind was filled with a yearning to protect what was mine.

This was crazy. I needed to go home. I need to take some time off.

Misha's eyelids fluttered. His blond curls slid across his pillow as he moved his head from one side to the other. He moaned and his lips formed a grimace.

As he slowly woke, I pressed my palm to his hand, covering it. I didn't think about the motion. My hand simply moved.

Our contact made my insides flare up, as if I were in the Burn. But I was not.

"You came back." Misha smiled through his pain, his pretty blue eyes still glazed.

"I find myself unable to leave your side."

"That's a problem, isn't it?"

The question sounded so innocent. But Misha was not impaired. He was intelligent. Highly intelligent. He knew what was going on as much as I did, perhaps clearer than I did because he would be without my denial.

"It is." I needed to be honest with him even if I had no answers.

"For the first time in my life, I'm sorry for what I am," he said.

"You should not be sorry," I said. Then I heard myself continue as if all the filters had been removed from my brain. And all sense. "You're the most beautiful person I've ever seen. A treasure. Smart, kind, with a bigger heart than anyone. You're a treasure. Misha, you're perfect."

"I'm not. I'm a monster and you shouldn't have ever touched me. You're marked by me and it can only harm you. I understand now why you need to stay away. You tried and now you must try harder."

Misha only wanted to love. He was made of love. He was life itself.

"You might see it that way, but I don't," I said.

Sylphs were too sensitive for this world. It was why they went mad. Why they often expressed themselves through violence. They felt everything around them with more sensitivity than the normal Alpha or Omega.

The post-pubescent Sylphs suffered a continual Burn. That meant all their senses were forever on high alert. That was their only crime. Nature had caused them to exist. At some point in our evolution after the females had all died out, they must have had a purpose. They had a place in society. But our history told nothing of it.

Misha gave me a soft smile, as if he'd been watching—and participating—in my thoughts all along. "There's nothing we can do about this. I know it. But why does it feel like a bond is forming?"

"You shouldn't worry so. That's my job." I couldn't tell him yet. He didn't need to know about my blood test and worry even more.

"This, what is happening with us, isn't your job," he replied softly. "I will always worry about you. Whatever you're thinking that you can't tell me. Whatever you're feeling."

"You need to try to think of other things."

"So do you. But you can't, can you, any more than I can?"

I shook my head.

"So now what? We suffer?"

I pressed my palm tighter against his hand and made no reply.

Suffering. The future looked to be filled with it. I'd already suffered when Mase was taken away from me. I'd been sixteen. Too young to Burn. Too young to form a real bond. But I'd never stopped feeling the pain of it.

Now this. What had I done to piss off all the gods?

And Misha? He deserved none of this.

My mind cried out with a thousand questions. There was an easy solution. Take Misha. Make him mine in the Burn. Bond with him. Why did it have to be any more complicated than that? I was an Alpha. I should have my way. I should be able to bond with whomever I wanted. Whoever called to my being. *Take what is mine!* Those words were part of the old oaths, from before modern civilization. From a time when Alphas, maddened by the Burn and the lust for a single Omega, battled in grit and blood and primordial urging to the death. Battled to claim what was theirs by right. No other Alpha could stop him except by death. Combat ended when only one heart was left behind and one Alpha stood amid the carnage of his claim.

If only it were that easy. Combat. Claims. They sounded straight-forward and uncomplicated even if they ended in bloody violence.

I was educated, well-mannered, even-tempered. I'd never had such thoughts!

I told myself my fantasies were getting away from me. That was all.

But it was more than fantasy.

I had the beginnings of a bond with this man. It was Mase all over again. An untouchable. A man who was unattainable, not an option. Yet again, I would have a prospective mate taken away from me.

I took my hand away from his and stood. "I need to go." It hurt to say those words.

"I don't want you to go," Misha said. "But I know you have to."

"I'm sorry."

I turned away. I heard him call my name once. I didn't look back.

Chapter Thirteen

Misha

"Geo!" I said.

But he didn't respond. He never looked back.

To watch him walk away hurt so much. More than the bruises and sprains. More than all the years of loneliness and isolation I had endured.

My arousal flared. There was nothing I could do about it.

I tugged at the restraints on my wrists. My sprained wrist in its splint shot pain up my arm.

I gritted my teeth and held my breath until the discomfort receded.

Lying back in my bed, I closed my eyes, willing myself to sleep. For a long time I lay awake, eyes closed, humbled by the emotional pain inside me that would never be comforted because I could never take a mate.

I didn't think about justice or fairness, but a few times, I'll admit, I lamented the fact that I was ever born. My upbeat personality rarely allowed me time for self-pity, but today I basked in it.

*

"Thank you," I said to the Omega who brought my dinner tray. He set it on the small table beside my bed, turned and shut my door behind him.

I heard the guards rattle the door knob as they used their key to lock it.

I had been out of the colony hospital for nine days, after spending two hooked up to an I.V. My neck and wrist were still sore, but I'd healed well.

I had not seen Geo since the second day in the hospital. Ten full days.

Tracy had thumped against my left wall all afternoon. Cedric moaned, calling out for me often, but I did not answer him. I stayed away from the hole between our rooms. If he peered in at me, I didn't know or care.

I leaned against the dusty windowsill and stared out at the green sea, and the wild meadows of my realm. I was a lost prince again under a terrible curse. My wealth was in the lands around me, in all that I could see, but could not help me.

I touched myself often, always in reverence and tribute to Geo. Did he know? Could he somehow feel me?

I tried to feel him in my mind. I knew there was something real there between us, the most sacred of connections. But he wouldn't admit it. And it would never be recognized by outside laws.

When I closed my eyes and focused, as I had done for the last few days, I saw Geo smiling, Geo leaning over me in the bath and running his soapy fingers down my thigh, Geo's dark green gaze running up and down my body heating not only my skin, which was always hot, always fevered, but the depths of my core, a place inside me that had been so hollow, so empty. Now a spark licked the void. Now a new and different warmth suffused my being from the inside out, and it didn't crave simple orgasms. It wanted a closeness of being, touch and talk, comfort and security. It wanted things I could barely describe but were emotional in content, the way wind and rain combined to make a force called a storm. The way imagination and play combined to make a story. I wanted. A thing. A feeling. A being. Though I was ignorant of such states, I instinctively knew to call it love.

I had time to think a lot. I wondered what would happen to all these feelings if Geo never came back. If he went into the

Burn, would I know? Would I be drawn to him until I clawed at my own skin? Would I go crazier to not be with him?

Sometimes, in the middle of the night, my fears became more amplified and I couldn't sleep. I couldn't self-soothe with masturbation. I could only lie in the dark and shiver at a misery that felt more far-reaching than any I had known in my sorry state of being a Sylph.

I would talk to the dark. "Geo, where are you?"

Only the thumps and cries of my brothers answered.

Chapter Fourteen

Geo

The weekend fell on the day after my last visit with Misha. I took it as an excuse to distance myself from everything that had happened at the colony. I would take the two days and force myself to break this bond with Misha. It was wrong. The bond risked my whole life. And it wasn't fair to Misha, for he could never leave, never have a real life.

The first thing I did on Saturday morning was check and double check my appointment at Zilly's chattel farm for my upcoming Burn. When my Burn arrived, I would lose myself in an Omega. It was right and proper and in the long-run it would be the best for Misha.

A tiny little bond could shatter if I worked hard enough at it. It had happened with Mase and could again. I was a pro at this. Bury myself in work and career, bury myself in young, cute Omegas during my Burn, and I was set.

That weekend I went for long jogs in the sun. I worked in my yard until sunset. I started heavy projects, like chopping down a dead tree that had been standing in the front yard ever since I moved in.

I exhausted myself until I collapsed into bed at night and fell into deep sleeps. But early in the mornings I'd be wide awake again, an erection stabbing the sheets and dreams of Misha lingering in the air around me.

By the time Monday arrived, I felt as if I'd had no time off at all.

I arrived at my office early, avoiding looking at the empty chair at Tory's desk.

I needed a new assistant and I dreaded the upcoming interviews.

I felt like I was slogging through mud to walk into my office, put on the coffee, and sit at my desk to face the work day. In every step I made through the colony, I could feel Misha in the air, on my skin, breathing him, smelling him, a blossoming sweetness, faint soapiness like the bubble bath I could never forget, and the constant heady and hot musk of his Sylph arousals.

It wasn't my imagination. I could sense it all.

The only updates I kept up with over the weekend concerning him were medical. I knew he'd left the hospital wing and been taken back to his room. I knew he was on lockdown as any Sylph would be who had hurt a member of staff. Misha had been the one who had been attacked, but it didn't matter. He'd injured an Alpha. He could no longer walk freely through the halls.

How I was going to continue to work here with Misha in the building, I didn't know. Already over the weekend my mind was searching out options. I would have to get a new job. That was a given.

But for now, I needed to stay at Riverside Colony a few more weeks. Along with that, I needed a new assistant.

When I turned on my computer I saw I had over four dozen messages. Slowly, I began to go through them. I had to read some twice to understand what they meant. That was how distracted my brain was, especially since half the messages concerned Misha.

My Misha. Much as I tried, he wouldn't leave my thoughts.

Several messages addressed Tory and his situation. I needed to sign off on Doctor Prim's reports. I saw that Tory had been taken to an institution for dangerous Alpha's to be mentally evaluated and, if need be, medicated.

Doctor Prim's reports on Tory stated he'd been recently divorced and not filed his status.

Unfortunately, it was an all-too often occurrence for bonded Alphas who divorced quite suddenly to suffer mental illness. Normally, bondmates would find it not only unethical, but physically painful to cheat on their husband. But in instances of abuse, arrest, illness leading to incapacitation, or death, many Alphas became unwillingly separated from their mates. If they weren't ready or agreeable to the status, they experienced wild and erratic hormonal changes that often led to self-destruction. Or worse.

Tory fell into that category. It was said his Omega had filed for divorce. I wondered what had happened. He had not reported his newly unmarried status, and therefore was not put on watch. His condition deteriorated. Though he did not conduct his business in person with Sylph patients, the moment Misha had become free to walk the floors of the first floor and enter my office unannounced caused Tory to have uncontrollable hormonal responses.

What was my excuse? I was unbonded. I was stupid to think Misha couldn't affect me, to think I was immune because of a residual fourteen year-old bond that was completely broken.

I'd tricked myself into thinking all was well with me. I was a fool.

And I'd let a Sylph wander the hallways free and unencumbered.

I did not deserve to work here.

The most recent message flashing at me was yet another from Doctor Prim. He wanted to meet with me in his office.

It was probably about my second blood test. I knew what it would say. The same thing. The beginning effect of a bond was blossoming in my veins.

I sent a quick message to him that I would meet him after lunch.

The morning went by slowly. My work suffered. So many forms, so much paperwork for the most insignificant things, orders for everything from new tires for the lawnmower to baby wipes. The colony needed to run like a smooth engine, every cog in its place, to keep up the level of care I demanded.

118

The changes I had made meant more paperwork, but when I'd first started the job I'd been up for it. Now, having lost my assistant, and unable to focus, I realized I was in over my head.

As I signed forms and answered mail, I was happy to see Misha had no charges brought against him for his self-defense against Tory. But I was not content that he'd been put on lockdown again. His freedoms had vanished. My new rules for him had been replaced with the old. It was a blow.

I ached for my Misha. I want to go to him. I clamped down on the urge and continued on with my work.

Lunchtime came and went. I had some fruit and more coffee. Then I set off to meet Doctor Prim.

There were only three patients in the colony's clinic today. It was a good day for health, I surmised.

Prim sat at his desk.

"Hello, sir." Prim, standing at his desk, motioned me to sit.

"After all we went through last week, you're still not calling me Geo?"

He smiled and some of his stern, no-nonsense business appearance was replaced with something real.

"Geo." He took a deep breath. "I have your labs back on the second blood test. Good news."

For a moment, my heart leapt. I needed good news. But then I realized this was about something forbidden. Taboo. Illegal. And it concerned my Misha. No matter what he said, it would not be good news.

"Let's have it," I replied, struggling to keep my voice calm.

"There is a bond forming. Things look good. Your tests were only three days apart, yet the bond has grown. It's a full point up. Three point nine out of a total ranking of ten. This is news I hope you are happy to hear."

My throat went dry. I swallowed to moisten it, then spoke. "Yes, thank you."

But it couldn't be. A bond that not only formed without sex, but was growing? The news startled me. There were Alpha and Omega couples who filed lawful bonds at that ranking. I expected Prim to say I still had residual bond elements in my bloodstream, the same or less. Not more.

Now Prim sat and leaned back in his chair, crossing his arms. He smiled again. "Misha is doing well. His wounds are quickly healing. Sylphs have odd metabolisms. Some heal fast, others not at all. It's a crapshoot sometimes. But Misha is the exception. He always has been."

I managed to nod my head.

"A fascinating Sylph, that one. He's one in a million. Defied all the odds," said Prim. "Everything about him is normal, including a few Alpha characteristics, except for his constant Burn. And a few other anomalies."

"What anomalies?" I asked.

He laughed. "His over-active imagination, for one."

"Anyone can have that."

"Yes, it's very sweet. In children."

"What else?"

"He doesn't knot, of course." Prim stated it as a fact, without emotion.

My cheeks heated. "Of course."

"His hormones are out of whack for either an Alpha or an Omega." Prim continued. "And he has control with the Burn, and zero violent tendencies. Even Tory's injuries were minor. He didn't need stitches at all. Misha is docile. Tame. He loves everyone he meets. For a Sylph, that is amazing."

"I noticed all of this when I met him."

"I don't condemn what you did, giving him more freedoms. I understand why. It was fair treatment. Misha had earned it. But you must keep in mind that Sylphs are not locked away simply to keep others safe. It's done foremost to care for them when they are unable to care for themselves."

"I know. I thought he'd be safe here, with an all bonded staff. I thought it would enrich him to have an expanded environment." I had hoped.

"You were right to think that. Of course he would be enriched. He is a delightful individual."

So, I thought. Even Prim had been affected by him. I wasn't alone. But Misha had not imprinted in Prim. He had imprinted onto me, and a bond began to form through something never before understood. Or if it was understood, it wasn't talked about, or written about in any textbooks I had seen.

My mind supplied the numerical figures of the bond again. A three point nine. That was too close to half of a full bonding for me not to realize it was forming into a full bond. I was already vulnerable to Misha and his effects. It would only continue to get worse.

"About my blood test. I've heard bonds cannot be broken except through death or divorce and re-bonding to another." Like with Mase. "Are there other ways? Maybe medical ways?"

Prim's eyebrows came together. "You aren't sure about this Omega, then?"

I could be honest about this answer. "I'm not."

"Medical intervention in a bond involves sedation, tricky for an Alpha, and must be closely monitored. If there are other ways, I don't know them."

I nodded, staying silent.

"Well, something is happening there, Geo," Prim said. "It should be a good thing. I wish the best for you."

"Thank you." I could tell he was curious about why I was asking these questions. But he said nothing.

I rose to leave.

Prim said, "Are you going to be seeing Misha today?"

"Not today."

When I walked back to my office, I kept wanting to divert to the elevator and go to the second floor. I had to force myself to stay on track.

I sat behind my desk the rest of the afternoon, most of that time with my head in my hands. Never in my life had I been one to make rash decisions. But I was facing one now.

I remembered my first Burn after I turned eighteen. Mase had been gone two years and it was still painful. I had cried for wanting him. The Omega who was servicing me didn't know what to do. I was convinced it was the worst first time an Alpha could go through. And that was with a partial bond that had been broken.

What I had with Misha was alive and growing. How would it feel to take another knowing I was leaving him behind, breaking our connection?

I had two weeks now before my scheduled Burn. Not enough time to plan anything, really, except defeat.

I stared at my blank computer screen for another hour before grabbing my jacket and calling it quits for the day. There was no use staying. I couldn't concentrate.

That night I found myself researching houses in Tarn, the country to the north. Just for fun, I told myself. Just to see what might be out there.

But I knew better. I wasn't researching fun. It was a fact that I would have to move far away. In Tarn, I could get a new start far from Riverside Colony. Distance was the answer. Distance and time for the bond to be broken.

I created a new file containing all the things I might need to get away and begin a new life. Start over. It felt good to be prepared even if it amounted to nothing.

In the file I added photos and links to the houses to the north. I gathered my financials to see what I might be able to swing. I was young, so I hadn't had time to invest much. But I had equity in my current home from which I could get a loan. I had modest savings. And I owned a fairly expensive car.

Also added to the file were two names. Mathias Vandergale. And Alden Norris. I'd gone to school with Mathias and we'd roomed together for two years. He was an asshole but a whiz at accounting. All kinds of accounting. He'd done a few scams in college and never been caught, or even suspected. I thought he was reckless and arrogant. His father was one of the richest men in the country. He didn't need the money. He did it for fun. He held a position on the board at Great East Bank due to his name. He might be able to help me get some quick money together.

Alden was worse than Mathias. He also went to the same college and dropped out his third year after he figured out he could sell his computer services, much of which included identity theft, for more than he could ever make at a legit job. Last I heard, he also worked for some underground organization, the kind of people you never wanted to piss off, let alone meet.

I told myself I wouldn't really connect with these men unless it came down to no more options, no more time. I had their names and contact information only to make myself feel more whole.

After a night of research, I went to bed tired. Misha, of course, was always on my mind. His smile, his pale eyes, his curls. His bubble bath scent. I had no rest from that. I fell to sleep thinking of him and woke the same.

My skin flamed but I wasn't in the Burn. I could feel it in my blood. Desire. I simply wanted him, I told myself. That was it. It had nothing to do with the Burn. Or if it did, it was his Burn I felt.

Whatever was happening between us, the barriers were falling lower and lower.

*

Alden stood behind the pawn shop counter looking decades older than when I'd last seen him, yet we were the same age. His thin brown hair was tied back in a ponytail, and he eyed me with the same smirk I remembered from our college days.

"How long?" I asked.

Alden flicked his thumb at the two photos and the thumb drive I'd provided. They sat on the chipped beige Formica countertop that looked like it hadn't been cleaned in years. The place smelled of oldness and dust.

"These suck. You need better photos," said Alden.

"Can't do it."

His dark eyes seemed to pin me. "I can work with the one. Not the other."

The photo of Misha was from his medical files. It was years old. He looked like a boy. I was only getting the new I.D. for him as a safe-guard. I had already decided not to take him with me in my new life, in my attempt to start over under a new name. It was only a matter of time before it was discovered that my bond was to a Sylph. Prim was smart. He'd figure it out. I couldn't stay. But the I.D. for Misha would be there if I changed my mind.

"Make it work," I said.

"It'll cost you more and take longer."

"We agreed on the price already. And I don't have longer."

"No can do, then," Alden said, turning away.

"Way to greet an old friend from college," I muttered.

He turned back to look at me. "We were never friends."

"Look. I'll throw in an extra five hundred. It's all I can spare."

"Why do you need all this? Why are you running? You were always such a pris-ass, Geo. Never broke the rules. Law-abiding. Upstanding. I deserve to know what the fuck's gone wrong."

"No you don't."

He frowned. "I'm connected. Maybe if someone is after you, I can help in other ways. No running. It might cost you more money, but cheaper and less inconvenient in the long-run."

"No."

"I don't owe you a god damn thing, Geo."

"It wasn't just Mathias who covered for you about those counterfeit hundreds you were passing in our sophomore year. I was there, too. Mathias may have used his Vandergale name and money to pay off the cops, but I lied to the cops, too. For you. I never told a soul."

"Yeah. Why didn't you?" Alden asked. "You hated me enough."

"I didn't hate you. Mathias was my roommate. You were his friend. I was afraid for all of us. And maybe I didn't like what you were doing, but I didn't want to see you go to prison. I didn't want to see anyone hurt over a few hundred dollars."

"Yeah, well thanks for your *compassion*." Alden drew the words out in pure sarcasm. "You're a little prick bringing all that up."

I stood and took his insults, forcing a calm I didn't feel. I waited. I wasn't going to beg, but beyond Alden, I had no other options for a fake I.D.

Alden stared at me. I glanced away.

He sighed. Out the corner of my eye, I saw him smile, but it didn't improve his look. It only made his smirk widen.

"Ten days is the best I can do," Alden finally said.

"Good." I checked my phone's calendar. "I'll be back on Thursday after next." I started to turn.

"Hey." He called me back.

"What?"

"I need *all* the money up front."

"Fine." I banged my briefcase onto the countertop and opened it. I took out two thick stacks of cash and placed them on the counter before him.

Swiftly, he grabbed up the stacks and stuffed them somewhere under the counter. I closed my briefcase and turned to leave.

A little bell on the front door jingled as I opened it.

We did not say goodbye to each other. Alden was right. We weren't friends.

*

I'd taken two days of sick leave which I didn't deserve since I was so new. There were so many changes I wanted to make to the colony, but it still ran itself as efficiently as any institution of its kind. No one had known during that time that I took a quick flight to Tarn and made inquiries into a small house there, ending up leasing it and stocking it all in one day. No one, not family or friends, knew what was going on with me, or how mortified I really was over this whole bond thing.

I'd been avoiding messages and phone calls, so when I got back to my office my inbox was bursting.

Slowly, I tried to go through them one by one, but my mind still wouldn't focus. Not only were thoughts of Misha continually haunting me, but all my secret plans for leaving had my stomach in knots. I couldn't eat. I couldn't sleep.

I wrestled with work for over an hour, downing three cups of coffee.

I only looked up when I heard the scuff of soft footsteps at my door.

Doctor Prim stood at the entrance to my office looking at me with a stare I couldn't read.

"Yes?" I put one elbow on my desk.

"Geo. Didn't you get my messages?"

"I've been out. I'm going through my inbox now."

"I see."

Prim came in and sat without being asked. He barely took a breath before making a simple, damning statement.

"We have some problems."

My hot skin went suddenly cold. "Is it Misha?"

I shut my mouth too late, realizing my fears had overridden my usual, rational self. With everything going on, I couldn't afford to lose it like this. I should have taken another sick day. I should have already put in my notice.

"Now why would you say that?"

I shrugged, tapping a few letters on my keyboard, pretending I was busy. Pretending I hadn't given away all my secrets with one thoughtless question about Misha to a man who already looked suspicious of me.

"Simply worried for a man who didn't deserve to be hurt," I said. "It's my job."

I knew I sounded overly defensive, but wouldn't any chief of staff in any institution feel the same?

"I *am* here about Misha," Prim replied. "But I am also here about you."

"Me?"

"May I ask why you took sick days for the past two days?" Prim asked.

"I wasn't feeling well."

"That's all?" he asked.

"That's all." I took my hands away from my keyboard and leaned back in my chair. "Why are you making what I do on my own time your business?"

"Because I'm filing my final report on Misha's condition and there are details in it that *are* your business. I've been putting it off for two days. Messaging and calling. You didn't answer."

"What details?" My heart pounded. My skin couldn't decide if the air in the room was too hot or too cold.

"Blood tests."

"And? What does that have to do with me?" I picked up my mug of coffee, realizing as it sloshed against the sides it was cold.

"I took it upon myself to run extra tests."

I bit the inside of my lower lip until I tasted salt. "You took it upon yourself?"

"Yes, sir."

The air between us nearly crackled. I did not take my gaze from his. I couldn't. The Alpha in me had reared up and it was pissed. All my defenses were up.

"Why would you do that?"

"Because I suspected."

I could have killed him where he sat. But I had expected no less from him. It was why my plans had been made in haste. I sat in forced calm and asked, keeping my voice low. "Suspected what?"

"The blood of the Sylph shows positive for a bond. Three point nine, in fact."

Time stopped.

"You fucked him," Prim said. I had never heard a crass word come out of his mouth until today.

"Of course I didn't!"

He continued as though he hadn't heard me. "It's taboo. It's against the law."

"I didn't do anything with him except befriend him!"

"You are lying and I understand why. Sylphs are irresistible to the unbonded. Tory didn't report his divorce. He felt it and the result was cataclysmic. You are unqualified for this job. You should not be chief of staff. You should never have been hired."

"I'm not lying! I never touched him in that way."

Prim's eyes squinted. "Why do you keep denying it? I have the blood tests. There is a bond. You lied to me about having an Omega partner where a bond was beginning. You lied about the effect Misha had on you when it should have been reported to me or another doctor at this facility right away."

"I didn't fuck him!" My voice came out in a yell.

Prim crossed his arms. "I must report this."

I looked down at my desk, finally breaking eye contact. I thought about my plans to move. Luckily, many of them were already in motion, but I needed more time.

"You seem like a good person. A smart person. I like you. This isn't personal. I am required by law to report any suspected breach by the staff. Especially impropriety with a patient. It's against the law!"

I met his eyes again. "I asked you the other day about breaking bonds. This was why. You don't have to believe me, but I never intended it. There was skin to skin contact between us, yes. But never sex. Never! I cared about him. But I never allowed it beyond that."

His eyebrows narrowed. "That's not possible. You are lying."

"I'm not. Don't you think I know it's impossible? That's why I was asking you all those questions and had you test my blood twice! I felt it happening but knew it to be impossible. If I were hiding something, I would never have come to you."

"A bond is created with knotting," the doctor began.

"With an Omega, it is, yes. I know that! But Misha's a Sylph. They're not Omegas. I didn't compromise myself! I certainly didn't knot him!" I gulped air, fuming.

Prim's lips flattened. He tilted his head. "If what you say is true, then—how?"

"I don't know! He fainted once when I visited him. I myself supervised him being taken to the baths. It was instinct. To help him regain his senses."

"He fainted? Why was I not called?"

"I didn't think it was necessary. Certainly the nurses on duty thought the same. They didn't call you, either."

"I am an expert in my field. I've worked here for fifteen years. I have never heard of a Sylph bonding. Never!"

"Me either. It's like Misha imprinted on me the instant we met. But more than that connected us. I don't know how. I'll admit I instantly cared about him. His plight is unusual. And unfortunate."

"It is unusual. I agree, but he is in danger. If what you're saying is true, then that proves it. He can never be free for the good of society."

"We tell ourselves that. We have all these laws in place that are supposedly for the good of society, of others. But Misha has fallen through the cracks. It isn't fair. All I wanted to do was help him."

"And you made him your personal project."

I couldn't deny it. "Yes."

Prim sighed. "For all I know about Sylphs, I will admit I have never known one such as Misha. Certainly, none who have been my patients have ever lived to age twenty. Never long enough to have even the most instinctive urge to bond. He's one to study. He's what people in my profession call a career-maker as far as studying him goes."

I waited, wondering where this was leading.

"You know I have to make my report. When I do, even if I do not mention your name, this facility will come under investigation. Everything and everyone will be tested and interviewed until they find an answer as to why a Sylph has formed a bond. He will be put through many tests, put under a microscope. Probably for the rest of his natural life."

"I understand you have to report this." As I spoke, I wondered if I could catch a flight out tomorrow. Another thought occurred. "Why have you held off? Why come to my office, accuse me, and warn me at all?"

Prim took a deep breath. "I do not condone what you have done."

I opened my mouth to protest. I'd done nothing but try to help the boy.

He held up his hand to stop me from speaking. "That said, I never said I didn't understand it. No one is perfect. My own bond with my Omega has withstood good and bad times. Don't get me wrong. We're happy and we adore our children. But I'd do anything for him. Anything. That said, I'm a doctor. My first obligation is to do no harm. I don't want to see you or Misha harmed."

My mind spun. The muscles in my face tensed. "What are you saying?"

"I will wait one week. This will give you a chance to get your affairs in order and, if you are ethically-minded, turn yourself in. Do you understand?"

130

I couldn't believe it. Prim was giving me yet another warning, but not the sort I'd expected. This one came with leeway, and time I sorely needed.

"Why?" I asked.

"I told you. *Do no harm.*"

It was a shock. If I had stayed working here longer, this rare Alpha and I might have become good friends. "I can't thank you enough."

"Don't thank me. You stand to lose everything."

I gave a tight nod.

Now, he would not look at me. "You have one week."

Beneath his ultimatum, I read the unspoken message. *You have time to run.*

Chapter Fifteen

Misha

Twelve days. I counted each day and night that passed without seeing Geo, repeating the number to myself over and over.

I'd expected repercussions after attacking an Alpha. I knew I'd done wrong. But I deeply wanted the chance to explain myself to Geo. I thought he understood. I thought he cared. He'd stayed with me almost constantly in the hospital after I'd awakened. He'd spoken to me gently. He'd touched my hand.

That touch. An unbonded Alpha's touch skin to skin! It sent me reeling. My body wanted to melt with the memory. I was so hot at times I thought I'd be reduced to ash.

Maybe it was best that Geo didn't come. I realized if I saw him I would not be able to control myself. I wanted him so badly I feared I would tackle him. I'd throw my arms around him. I'd yell. I'd weep.

I had no more control.

Would he hate me for it?

But my questions were a waste of energy. He didn't come to see me and he probably never would.

I hated him for staying away. I loved him and it hurt.

Everything hurt. The sounds of the castle were no longer comforting. Tracy's thumps and Cedric's cries made my ears ache. The food smelled rotten. My bed was lumpy. Every touch to my skin flamed and stung. Light stabbed my eyes. My sleep was invaded by Geo, good dreams and nightmares both.

I stopped going for exercise. When my guards came by to take me to overlook my realm, I told them to go away. I told them I didn't feel well. That brought the nurses. Eventually, it brought a visit from Doctor Prim, who'd already given me a clean bill of health the week before, and had set up appointments with the resident therapist.

That therapist did nothing much more than give me tests. Lots of computer tests that required answers to difficult and very personal questions.

When Doctor Prim entered my room, I got a whiff of Geo, faint, then gone. Had they been together? Talking? More?

I was instantly jealous before I realized, smelling the doctor, that his bond was strong and his pheromones normal. He had the peaceful scent and content nature of all the bonded doctors, nurses and guards who came into contact with me. Tory had been the only one who'd smelled different. And, of course, my king, Geo.

"Misha. How are you feeling?"

I wasn't feeling well but I didn't want him to know. So I lied.

"Fine."

Doctor Prim came forward. He reached out with his gloved hands and lifted my chin. "The bruising is nearly gone. Any pain?"

"No."

"Good. How's the wrist?"

"Fine."

The doctor held up a tablet. "I have some test results from your therapist. Instead of having him go over them, I thought I would, since I needed to clarify some things."

I nodded, unsure his reasoning made any sense but unwilling to question him on it.

"Good." He went to the door and spoke.

A guard brought in a chair and Doctor Prim sat, motioning for me to sit on my bed.

"Did I do something wrong on the tests?" I asked.

"No. Not at all." He scrolled through some pages on his tablet. "Let's see. Here, I just want to make sure about this, when you were asked if any impropriety has ever occurred toward you in this institution, you answered no. I'm double checking on that, because obviously you suffered an Alpha attack."

"I wasn't thinking about that when I answered."

"But the attack had just occurred. Surely that would be fresh on your mind."

"When I saw the word impropriety, I thought it meant sexual misconduct."

Prim nodded. "I see. And so you were answering that nothing like that has ever happened to you?"

"Yes."

Prim was silent a moment. I realized he was looking for another answer. Or perhaps an admission from me that I was lying.

"If you're asking if I'm a virgin, then my answer is yes. I am," I added.

One of his dark, sleek eyebrows rose.

I continued. "I have had no contact with anyone but bonded Alphas and Omegas."

"You had contact with Geo. He is unbonded."

My face grew more heated. I wondered if the color changed enough for Doctor Prim to notice. I was always hot, always in the Burn, so maybe he would see it as normal.

"He's a friend. He'd never harm me," I finally answered.

"Of course. But there were times when you both came into contact, skin to skin, I mean."

Where was he going with this?

I thought again about the day I'd been so overwhelmed I'd fainted. How Geo had carried me to the baths and placed me in a tub. He'd bathed me until he became very uncomfortable and couldn't finish. Geo was a good man. I wanted him badly. I loved him. He had responded but he had also restrained himself.

"Geo is a man who has great control. He helped bathe me one day when I was sick. I responded and he never once took advantage of that. Why are you asking me these questions?"

"Ah, just routine."

"It's not routine. Is Geo in trouble?" My heartbeat increased. My throat went dry. "Is that why he doesn't visit me anymore?"

My insides felt shredded at the idea that maybe he no longer even worked here. I'd never have hope of seeing him again. Heat pulsed behind my eyes at the horror of that thought.

"Nothing for you to worry about." Prim's voice was kind, controlled. His lips curved up slightly. "The protocol of wearing gloves while treating patients is a minor infraction."

I thought about the times he'd touched me, skin on skin, in the colony hospital. Had Prim seen?

"I didn't think about it. That he touched me. But he didn't harm me. He never would. I don't want him to get into trouble because of me!"

Prim opened his mouth to speak. I interrupted him.

"He's only ever been fair and kind to me. He listened to me in ways no one ever has when I talked. He cared that I might be more than capable of participating in some sort of life routine outside this locked room."

"You called him your king."

I let out a half-laugh. "I did. And I'm a Sylph prince who sits in wait in his castle by the green sea until he comes of age and can inherit his destiny."

Prim swallowed. His dark eyes seemed to bore into me.

"What else am I supposed to do with all this time locked away but create a life for myself?" I continued. "I can read and learn and watch TV only so much. Your life is what you make it, don't you think? Well, I'm a prince. And by whose law can you say I am not? Yours? I don't live in your world, Doctor."

"You're very articulate."

"I don't know what to say to that."

"I'm saying that I am impressed with you. And I do not for one moment condemn Geo for taking an interest in you. But there is something you must understand. And I know you do. Geo does not live in your world. Nor you in his. He must obey other rules and laws."

He was a king from a visiting kingdom with a different culture from my own. I understood that. Geo had to answer to other authorities I'd never know.

"This means," Prim continued, "that he cannot do for you the things he might have wanted to try. He might want you to have more freedom, but he puts his own career and life in jeopardy by trying to give you those things. He can harm himself if his judgment is impaired."

Shock ran through my system in bursts of sharp adrenaline. Had my behavior somehow harmed Geo?

I got up and started pacing the small space by the window. "I don't want him to ever come to harm."

"You want him, though."

I didn't answer.

"If you act on your feelings, he will come to harm. Do you want that?"

I paced faster. The room blurred. "I didn't. I haven't. I would never hurt him!"

"I know that, Misha."

It was the first time I heard him use my given name.

"You're not like the others. You can control yourself in the Burn. You can control your desires. You can control how you express your love."

I loved everyone I met, I told myself. I loved Geo, too. But it was more than that. If my body burned, it burned for him. All the time. It was about him and no one else, not even about myself and my own Sylph needs. My inner being glowed for Geo.

It was the connection between us. It was like a real Alpha/Omega bond, except I wasn't an Omega or an Alpha.

Did Doctor Prim suspect this connection? Did he know more than he was saying?

"If you care about him—and I know you do; you're a compassionate soul—you will never act on your feelings for him. You will send him away if he comes to you. Always. Do you understand what I'm saying?"

I nodded. "But he hasn't come to me since the hospital. I swear it." A tear like a singe of ash hit my cheek. "He won't come. I can feel it in my heart."

"Understand this, if he does. If he tries to see you, or get you to do anything outside of your routine, you must resist him."

"Why would he—?" I stopped. I didn't want to finish that question because I didn't want to know the answer.

"For his own safety, for his own good, you must not see him. You must not allow his touch ever again."

"Why are you saying all this?" Now more tears blinded me.

"Because from what I have seen of Geo, and what I know of him, he might try to see you. He's compassionate and caring. But he does not deserve any harm. He has not done wrong. But our world won't see it that way if you, either of you, see each other ever again. Our world will punish him."

"The world doesn't know anything." My breath hitched. "Does it?"

"I have reports to file. Things may come to light. Geo will be all right, but if he tries to see you, resist him. I cannot emphasize this enough. Do not allow it. It is for his own safety and his own good."

I blinked hard and Doctor Prim came back into focus. He was standing now, facing me, reaching out. He put his gloved hand on the side of my face.

"Press all those feelings back inside you. I see them. You can't hide them from me. Hold them down. Tight. Don't let go of them. Lock them away. You're a good person in an unfortunate circumstance. But you can still do more good. Cut him off in your mind."

How could he know what I was feeling and for whom? But he spoke as if he could read my mind, as if he'd been confessed to and was an advocate for Geo. Had Geo sent him?

"Promise me," he said.

I couldn't speak. It was too painful. I closed my eyes and pretended for a moment I was a prince again, and the realm depended on me, as well as the stranger king who needed my help.

I imagined myself standing outside the wire fence an hour after a storm and the grass was so green and sparkling it hurt the eyes. The clouds were like lacy scarves, fading. Roses bloomed at the edge of a small road. Vines covered the trunks of trees overflowing with supple, new leaves.

My kingdom was beautiful and I needed to preserve that. Its purity, its rich textures and scents, its soul. My kingdom came from deep within me and contained all my love and hope. All my devotion.

Geo was part of that and I could never allow him to come to harm.

I opened my eyes, now sticky with tears. Doctor Prim stood before me, his eyes serene but dark, firm in his convictions. He waited for my answer. It had to be the right one.

"I promise," I said.

"Good."

When he left and the door to my room closed and I heard the lock set, I crumpled to my knees.

I heard Tracy thumping harder than ever against one wall. I heard Cedric's howling and through the other. Their songs soared through me. I joined them.

My fists pounded against my pretty brown floor. My voice rose, part shriek, part sob, part howl.

I'd made a promise and I'd keep it. But it hurt. It hurt so bad.

I would never see my king again.

Chapter Sixteen

Geo

Mathias was a hard man to see. He had people. And his people wanted to talk to my people, only I didn't have any. He was far too busy and important to answer my texts, or the messages I left on his service.

I wondered if he even remembered me.

Time was passing by too quickly. I needed to get everything on my checklist done.

When we finally connected and we agreed to meet, I worried I had no time left to accomplish what I needed for a clean break at a new life.

It had been six years since I'd seen him. We'd been roommates for the first two years of college even though he could certainly have afforded his own place. The last two years of school, we'd stayed friends attending the same parties, hanging out with the same crowd even though he was a richer than all of us put together.

Now he walked into the meeting room at the bank as if he owned the place—which perhaps he did, or his father did—and he was more beautiful than ever.

Always in college he'd gotten his way in everything because of his money and his looks. His black hair glowed, absorbing all the colors of any room he entered. He wore it long in a single braid. He was tall and lean and his suit fit him probably better than the model who'd worn it on the runway. In fact, he'd probably bought it for thousands of dollars right off the model's body.

Mathias was like that. He had the best of everything and expected it, too.

At thirty, he was more breathtaking than ever. I might've had an Alpha-Alpha crush on him in school if he'd shown any heart at all. If his dark eyes weren't so hard and the words from his mouth so foul. And if his gazes when they raked my body weren't so full of frozen ice.

"So," he said, walking into the bank's second floor meeting room. "You need my help." No preliminaries. No *how are you*. Just straight to the point.

"Nice to see you again, too, Math," I replied.

He made a little grunt. "It's kinda funny, you coming to me like this."

"Why is that?"

"I never figured you for a guy who needed anyone, really. You stayed to yourself like you were just too good. The good good boy."

"Yeah," I said. "Well, here I am."

He looked me up and down. Eyes depthless, hollow. He was fine, so fine, but I really wondered if he had a soul.

"So you need a fast liquidation?"

It sounded terrible, somehow. I almost said no. But I nodded yes.

He shrugged as if it were no big deal and sat at the head of the conference table. "I'm your guy."

"I can't pay your fee right now."

He frowned up at me. "Sit." Then he chuckled. "Idiot, you think I need money?"

"I don't know, but I can pay. Just later. When I get re-settled."

"You don't have to pay. But maybe I'll ask *you* for a favor some time, how's that?"

I stared at him, frozen. What did that mean?

Mathias chuckled again. "Just kidding. I'm happy to help out my old roommate. We had some good times, yeah?" His eyes sparkled now. There was something alive there, then. For real.

"Yeah."

I handed him my financial file. He looked it over and pulled open his laptop lid. He typed for a while, then snapped the lid shut.

"There," he said.

"What?"

"Done."

"Everything?"

"All your money from your 401k is transferred to your account. Your other accounts have been combined. I made a note for them to have all the money in cash waiting for you, no questions. We pride ourselves on our privacy here." His grin was almost wild. "And the taxes for early withdrawal on retirement won't need to be filed until next year, so fuck it, right? Damn, it's not much money, though. I mean, really, Geo, you said you're moving to Tarn. I haven't even asked you why but I figure knowing how smart you are, it's for a good reason. Do you need more money?"

"I have my house."

Mathias re-opened his computer. "Address?"

I gave it.

"It's got some equity. I can get you credit on it. I can arrange the sale of it for you later. I've got friends in real estate."

"Cash credit?" I asked.

Mathias snorted. "Fuck, you are going dark, eh? I'll make it happen but that might take a few days."

"I'll be gone by tomorrow."

Mathias took a deep breath. "Here's what you do. Contact me when you get where you're going. Will there be people after you?"

I shrugged. If I was caught for forming a bond with a Sylph, a judge could sentence me to anywhere from a year to five years prison time. There would be a warrant out on me at the very least.

"They might freeze all your assets once they know you're gone. I'll make sure this is hidden for a while. I'll have the money wired."

"Don't. Not if it will get you caught." I didn't want Mathias mixed up in this.

Mathias flung me one of his full, perfect white-toothed smiles. "Sweetheart, former roomie-of-mine, I never get caught."

As he leaned back, arms behind his head, he said, "Look, I don't know what's up with you. I don't care. But you were a good roomie. You covered for Alden when all that shit went down. And you knew about some of my own youthful indiscretions. And you never said a word. You let me know if you need more money. My father has more than there are drops of water in the sea."

"I don't need--"

"Don't be proud, Geo. You're always so proud. I know you're not an asshole. You'd never ask. You would never take advantage. But those years in college were okay. You're like a brother. You remind me of--"

He stopped. He pounded his fist on the tabletop as if to chase away some other sort of pain, then said, "Are we done then?"

I nodded. But I knew what he was going to say. He'd gotten really drunk one night back in college and told me in almost the same words, voice low, words slurred. *Geo, you remind me of my fucking litter-mate. Kris. What a fuck-up. I did him wrong, damn it. But hey, if you ever tell anyone I said that I'll deny it.*

At the time, I didn't know whether to take it as a compliment or not that he had compared me to his brother. But today, I saw. He was helping me partly for himself. He was making up for something. Maybe some bad deed. Something to do with Kris, who I knew nothing about and had never met. Litter-mates were usually very close. If he'd wronged one, well, even someone as hollow as Mathias might occasionally feel the tiniest twinge of guilt. Especially while drunk.

"Thank you, Math."

"Mouth shut. This meeting didn't happen. Thanks not necessary." He stood and looked down at me with his eyebrows narrowed. "I'd wish you luck but you're too smart for that. You don't need it. You may not be street-smart but you'll learn fast."

Before I could get out of my chair and get to the door he was gone, laptop under one arm, sauntering rapidly down the long, plush hall of the bank's main office complex.

I went to the downstairs teller window, collected my cash which was nicely done up in bundles. It had been placed in a leather case which I knew wasn't standard and had to have been also authorized by Mathias.

I had a rental waiting for me when I got outside, the first use of my new credit card under my false I.D. from Alden. I'd sold my car yesterday and taken the train into the city this morning.

On my two hour drive home I battled second-thoughts until I was talking to myself, yelling in the closed space of the vehicle. All the voices looking to be heard inside my head came out. They called me insane. They called me all the words for idiot that Mathias might never have thought of.

But one thing they couldn't diminish. The draw, the longing, the primal ache from deep within that demanded I take what was mine and make him my mate.

Nothing, no logic, no threat, no idea of failure could extinguish that flame.

I had decided over a week ago not to take Misha with me. Now I faltered.

I need to make a final call on this. I needed to stand by my convictions. And I had no time left. Either I would leave alone tonight. Or take what was mine. Could I do both?

Chapter Seventeen

Misha

I had cried so many tears over the next few days my pillow was wet.

The fate of Geo, which I had thought at first was personal, might have involved more than Doctor Prim had hinted at. The nurses and guards had started gossiping. I overheard mostly snippets about his work hours.

"Geo only came for a half-day three days in a row."

"Geo was out for two days plus the weekend and Jamie who works in the hospital said it was for his Burn."

"Geo was off all day yesterday. Again!"

My primary road to comfort was my imagination. I told myself a story.

King Geo had left on matters urgent to the realm. There were battles to be won and lost. He might never return. But if he did return, for the safety of himself and his kingdom, I could never be seen with him. I could not communicate with him, for unfortunately, my own people would see it as an act of treason. I would be condemned, but worse, King Geo might find himself in the middle of a full rebellion.

I would never risk his life for my own personal gain. My wants and desires must be ignored at all cost, however much it pained me.

Three nights after the visit from Doctor Prim, I lay on my bed in the darkness, eyes wide open, the shadows so thick I couldn't see my hand in front of my face. My tablet was at my side. I'd already checked it twice in one hour for the time. It was only just after midnight. The night that would never end.

I kept telling and re-telling my story in my mind, emphasizing the parts where my king's life hung in the balance and my own desires would seal his fate.

My mind brought his image to me in full three-d color. I saw his dark lashes framing sweet green eyes, his strong mouth and jaw, his rich brown hair in two distinct curves framing his forehead. His lean body in a crisp white shirt promised all sorts of planes and dips and valleys if I could only reach out, remove that shirt and touch him. I knew his skin would be soft, prickly with brown hair in all the right places, and hot, so hot.

For a long time I let my little fantasy play out, knowing it was wrong. I needed to deny myself any thoughts like that. I must not let my feelings for Geo rule me.

I concentrated on the footfalls of the night guard walking up and down the hall every few minutes. I counted his steps. Thirty up. Then he would vanish for about five minutes. Then thirty back toward my area of the hall.

For once, both Cedric and Tracy were quiet. Sleeping. I heard a few distant echoes, cries of the afflicted like me, but so far away as to be mere whispers.

I counted the guard's steps again and again. When he was gone a little longer than I thought he would be, I realized I'd fallen into a doze and missed his next round.

My body raged under the sheets, wanting, always wanting.

My mind called for Geo. My blood flamed for him. The Burn created in me a nearly unstoppable force. I felt so weak before it. How could I ever stop wanting Geo?

Again he appeared in my mind and would not leave.

His scent drifted over me, hair gel that smelled like sweet warm leather, clothing emanating the freshness of the wind, the Alpha spice that was almost animal, feral and charging and strong. I wanted it to take me. Take me away.

As I breathed in the scents of my imagination, I marveled at how good I was at making it real. I felt him as if he were in the room, close, so close.

I heard the footsteps of the guard again and began to count them to distract myself. One, two, three. They sounded a little lighter than usual. Had there been a shift change? But that usually happened at five a.m.

These weren't the usual guard's boot steps. I convinced myself it must be a nurse. Until they stopped right outside my door.

I heard the lock on the door rattle and unlatch.

I sat up, the sheet pooling at my thighs.

No nurse would be checking in on me at this time of night unless I was screaming bloody murder.

The door opened.

I blinked at the faint gold light coming in through the door and there he was. Impossible. Wrong. Forbidden.

My king?

My Geo had returned to me!

I sat up in my bed.

"Good. You're awake," he whispered.

"What?"

"Shh!"

Geo came into the room and I pulled the sheet with me as I scrambled toward the head of my bed. "No! You can't be here!"

The drifting scent of him, all leather-sweet and spice. It hadn't been my imagination at all. I'd smelled him coming probably from the moment he'd entered the castle.

"I am here," he whispered. "And we don't have long."

"Long? Long for what?"

"Just in case, put these on." He held up a pair of cuffs, glinting and glowing in the dim light. I could see he had on no gloves.

I looked up at him. "What are you doing?"

He looked at me for a long moment before replying. "You're being moved."

"I am?"

He nodded. "Come on. Get up. Get dressed."

146

I started to push back the sheet before I remembered Doctor Prim's words. I couldn't see Geo anymore, the doctor had said. It would hurt us both. If he asked me to do anything out of routine, I should decline him.

"If I really am being moved, the nurses and guards can take care of that," I said.

He took a step forward and my skin tingled. My cock hardened tight against my belly. "No, don't come any further."

He frowned. "What? Misha, it's only me. Why are you afraid?"

"I just can't go with you. If you're asking me, then I say no. Send a nurse." I brought the edge of my sheet up to my face and hid behind it, peering out over the top.

He looked so good standing there, like a hero come to take me away. Like a real king. But it was wrong. Doctor Prim told me. He'd been stern. I could feel that he'd been scared, too.

No, something was off. Something was bad. I didn't care about myself. I cared that Geo might be hurt.

"Geo, you have to go away." My voice came out all shuddery and weak. I had to be strong. But I wasn't. Not with Geo. I sucked in a deep breath.

He lowered his eyes and turned his head as if to look over his shoulder. There was a guard out there somewhere and I could smell that Geo was afraid.

"I don't have time to explain, Misha. But come with me now, and I'll tell you everything."

"I can smell it in the air. You're lying. You're doing something wrong. It's too dangerous. Geo, you have to go." My lips trembled as I spoke those words.

Geo said something that sounded like a curse under his breath. He never cursed that I had ever heard. He rapidly took three steps forward to the side of my bed.

I pressed myself back against the wall, my heart hammering.

Then he reached out. I thought he might grab me, well, not really, for he'd never hurt me, but I didn't know what he might do.

But all that happened was he touched the side of my face with his naked palm, gentle and warm, his thumb slowly stroking down my cheek.

He glanced behind his shoulder again. When he didn't see anything, he leaned forward and kissed me on the forehead.

"Please. Get dressed."

The touch against my cheek was bad enough, but that kiss. Soft lips above my brow. Warm breath. The nearness of him, of my Geo made everything inside me want to flame and melt and explode all at once. I wanted to kneel at his feet, beg him for—what? Everything. Anything he would give me. The instinct was strong. Too strong for me.

Doctor Prim's words came back to me, but as whispers now. Barely heard.

I pushed the sheets away and stood naked before my king. My voice shook as I said, "All right, Your Grace. But why am I being moved?"

A strained smile pushed at his lips. "It's all good, I promise."

He picked up my jumpsuit from where it lay across the foot of my bed and handed it to me.

I loved him but I didn't yet trust him. It wasn't about me. It was about him. What he was doing was against all the rules. He wasn't hurting me, he was hurting himself.

I shrugged quickly into the jumpsuit, fastening it and turned to look at the cuffs he held in his hands.

"Turn around," he said. "These are to protect you if we are seen."

I obeyed, placing my hands behind my back. He put the metal rings around my wrists. They were cold against my skin. Hard and unyielding.

"Why am I being moved?" I asked again.

"For your protection," he answered.

148

I had no time to process any of what was going on as he took me by the arm and pulled me into the hall.

I blinked hard in the brighter light, trying to see if anyone was about, a nurse, a guard, anyone. But it was silent. The long hall was empty.

"Your Grace, if I may speak."

He tugged harder, pulling me alongside him, obviously in a hurry.

"I have no shoes," I said when he didn't answer.

"You don't need shoes right now. I'll have shoes for you where you're going."

"You will?"

"Yes."

Geo led me all the way down the hall. The nurse's station was dark for the night. The night crew operated from the hospital wing which stayed open twenty-four hours. I knew that from my briefly allotted freedoms when Geo had first come to the castle.

We went all the way to the elevator where Geo pushed the *down* button.

I knew where we'd end up. On the first floor near his office. There were guards by the front door. I'd seen them before. We'd be caught for sure and Geo would have to explain why he had me with him in the middle of the night.

When the elevator doors opened, I pulled back from him as he tried to lead me inside.

"I'm afraid."

"You don't have to be," he replied softly.

Tears welled in my eyes. "You'll get caught. If you're doing what I think you're doing, you'll get caught and then you'll be hurt and I can't think about that. I can't!"

"Shhh." He stood on the threshold of the elevator and put his hand on the side of my head, fingers combing through my curls. "I've been planning this for almost two weeks," he said.

Two weeks? "I—I don't understand."

149

"Misha, you have to trust me."

He was my king. And an Alpha. If I couldn't trust him, then who could I trust? I thought about Doctor Prim and his warnings. But did I trust Prim? I didn't even know the man.

I wanted to go with Geo. I wanted it with all my heart. But if it led to something bad, I couldn't take it.

"I do trust you, but--"

"Come with me."

I stepped into the elevator with him and held my breath all the way down. When the doors opened I hesitated again.

What about the guards by the front? What if they saw us?" I was trembling now.

"Misha."

I looked up, realizing I'd stopped moving. Eyes wide, I stepped into the corridor and glanced toward the front of the building. There was low lighting, lots of shadows and no guards.

I looked at Geo.

"How?"

"Don't ask questions. Just do as I say."

The hospital on the first floor where most of the night staff worked was located around the corner and down another hall, far enough away from Geo's office to not be seen.

In my bare feet and jumpsuit, cuffed and with Geo's hand on my elbow, we walked through the double glass front doors and to the outside of the castle.

Trumpet vines grew on lattices along the walls, and yellow forsythia bloomed against the long porch wall. I could smell the freshness of the night air on the dewy grass.

"Come," Geo said softly.

He led me down the front path to a parking lot and a car. Quickly, he opened the front passenger door and pushed me inside.

I had never been in a car before. I'd seen them. I'd watched them on videos. But now I was in one, and it was going to roll away with me inside and Geo driving.

My hands shook. I felt like I'd lost all feeling in my body. This wasn't happening. This couldn't be happening.

Geo ran around to the other side of the car and got in, starting it up. It rumbled to life. A faint vibration passed through my seat and on the floor under my bare feet.

"Ohhh," I breathed.

"Okay?" he asked.

"No." I swallowed hard.

"It's all right, Misha. I'm a good driver."

"I am sure you are." I turned to look at him. "So, you're taking me away, then? Just like that?"

He said nothing, pulling out of the parking space. I wasn't prepared and my head slammed back on the soft head-rest.

"Geo, you can't do this."

"But I am. And you came willingly with me, right?"

I nodded hesitantly. It was true. But it wasn't fair. I couldn't resist him when he was in this mode. His Alpha scent was triple strong compared to when we first met. His Burn was coming on. I could smell it and what made it worse was the fact that he was unbonded. And the way he took charge commanding me, though gentle, made him irresistible to me.

I wasn't Omega but I wasn't Alpha, either. In Geo's presence, I simply responded. As a Sylph. For me that meant a dire urge to mate, to bond, to make him mine, for my Burn never receded, never rested.

My whole body gave a shudder from my toes to the top of my head.

"I have food in the back in a cooler. I have pillows. You can get some sleep if you want."

I turned to him, watching his profile dimly lit in the lights from the dash. "Where are we going?"

"It's some distance. We'll be driving all the rest of tonight."

"And there we'll be safe?"

"Yes."

"And together?"

"Yes."

"Geo?"

He turned his head slightly, listening.

"You've lost your whole career for me. Your life here. Everything."

"No. I haven't. I'm young. I can start my career over. What I've done is gain a life. You. I was nothing before I met you. It may have taken me awhile to realize it but it's right. It feels whole now."

"But we barely know each other."

"That's the thing. We do. In here." He tapped the side of his head. "A bond has been forming since we met. I know you feel it."

A bond? Of course I felt a connection. But was he actually confirming a bond? I had to be dreaming. "I do feel it. Even now. But I thought it was my imagination."

"It's real."

"But we never had sex. Don't you have to have sex to form a bond? And I'm not an Omega. No one knows if Sylphs *can* bond."

"They can. I have the blood tests to prove it."

"You didn't tell me this."

"No and I'm sorry. Apparently, skin to skin contact between us was sufficient. That, and maybe it's as simple as being superbly compatible. That fact is not in any text. I was ignorant. But I'm still to blame. I wasn't careful. For that I'm sorry."

"No, you were not careful." Nor was I. "But I'm not sorry." I paused. "You have blood tests, you said?"

"Yes."

"Mine as well?"

"Yes."

"The bond is truly real?"

Geo caught his lower lip between his teeth. He kept his eyes on the road, but his right hand reached over to me and touched my wrist. "Yes."

I moved my hand up and curled my fingers around his. "So that's why Doctor Prim came to see me."

"What?" He shifted in his seat. "He came to see you?"

"He told me you might be in danger and the way I could help protect you was to do my best to reject all my feelings for you." Now, as I spoke those words, they sounded cruel. But I still believed he was trying to help Geo. "I wondered how he knew. He told me I would do great harm to you if I allowed my feelings to continue. I believed him."

"He ran the blood tests. He knew and he respected me enough to give me time to put things right and leave my job. But he didn't take into account that when I left I wasn't going to leave you behind. I thought about it for a long time, but realized I could never do that. Never. An Alpha does not leave his mate."

My heart thumped hard at the word *mate*.

"He should have known that," Geo continued. "Maybe he thought the bond wasn't strong enough, or that it could be undone by distance and will power alone."

"You see me as your mate?" I could not believe I'd heard him correctly.

"I do."

Ecstasy coursed through me. "I tried to not think about you. But I could feel you all day and all night." I paused, glancing at him, my body drumming with blood and heat. "You're very close to a Burn now, aren't you?"

He nodded.

I smiled. "I can help."

"I know you can. But I want you do know I don't just want you because of the Burn." His voice softened. "I couldn't stop thinking about you, either. It's as if I had always known you but didn't know it. My body and mind were waiting for the moment you crossed my path. I simply never realized it. It was you I wanted, Misha. Just you."

I wasn't sure. We Sylphs have seductive ways, and chemical essences that powder the air. Our skins are potent. What if this was still only the Sylph allure, and we'd wake up tomorrow as strangers to each other?

"Maybe you're simply under my spell," I said, gripping his hand tighter.

"If I am, I hope that spell never breaks."

It was the sweetest thing I'd ever heard. My chest constricted. My lungs shivered with escaping air.

Geo's soft voice broke through my response, the sound bringing me even more pleasure.

"I honestly thought I would be all right working at the colony. I had a residual bond long broken that made me not want any other bond, possibly for the rest of my life."

"I know. I smelled it on you. You told me at our second meeting it was a partial bond. But you said nothing more."

"When I was sixteen it happened. Before my first Burn."

At age sixteen? "But you were just a kid, then!"

He nodded. "His name was Mase and he was an Omega. He was sent away to bond and marry another. I didn't speak for year afterward."

"Oh, Geo."

"It caused my sex drive to be lowered. I had no desire after that for a bondmate or family. I thought my condition would allow me to safely work at Riverside. I never thought I'd meet any Sylphs that weren't still children. I never thought I'd meet you."

I bowed my head and pressed my lips tight. I'd cried enough in the past two days. I wasn't going to let myself go again.

"I'm so sorry about your first bonding," I said, feeling his pain within me as if it had happened to me.

"Me, too."

I sensed he didn't want to speak of this anymore. I took a deep breath. "Where are we going?"

"Tarn."

"And that's where we'll live?"

"Yes."

"How will we disguise me being a Sylph?"

"I have that covered somewhat. We'll work on it together. People must think you're my Omega. But mostly, for now, you're going to stay away from people. I hate to do that to you--"

"No, it's all right. I'm used to it. Besides, if I have you, I don't need anyone else."

Our hands never let go, even after I grabbed a pillow from the back and fell asleep against Geo's shoulder. For hours he drove one-handed until we had to stop for gas.

Later, after eating a sandwich, I fell asleep again as the sun rose in pink hues through the windshield, warming my face.

Chapter Eighteen

Geo

I had a checklist that seemed a mile long. I'd managed in less than two weeks to get everything on it done.

Now I was hyped up, my body stiff and tight, my breaths short. I could feel my heart racing.

Driving helped calm me. With Misha asleep at my side, and his warm, sweet scent filling the air, everything seemed all right. No matter what, having him with me made my world whole. I didn't care about anything else.

He was right to insinuate I could be driven by the Burn. That this act of taking him away from the only home he'd ever known was a meaningless response to outside stimuli that might end after the mad heat of the time was over.

But I wouldn't let that happen. First, I wanted him and I didn't care about anything but that. The Alpha in me had finally awakened, as if I'd been stuck in some loop in time that kept me on low-drive, kept me in a sort of frozen state where my Burns were low-key compared to other Alphas I knew. It kept my life revolving around school and work since I'd turned eighteen.

Nothing wrong with work. People made decisions all the time to focus on career and little else. It brought security, money, and even a form of happiness for the job well-done. I was okay with all that, though it did make me feel a little old.

Beyond Mase, I'd never been in love. I remembered my feelings for Mase, and they were sweet and wonderful, but they were nothing like what I felt toward Misha.

I truly did not believe I could feel this strongly again on any level. Now, I wanted nothing else. I didn't have any misgivings or guilt about taking Misha away from Riverside Colony.

It was nice that as the chief of staff I could override the cameras at the elevators and front doors. I had tricked the night guards into doing a short project for me, then simply walked in and stole Misha. It was far easier than it should have been.

Knowing Mathias and Alden had paid off, too.

Did I regret that I was leaving my job? My career?

A little bit.

But Misha deserved everything and I realized in this final past week while making my plans, that I would do anything for him. I told myself a doctor does no harm. I was a therapist and had taken the same oath. To help him, to keep him from further harm, I was giving him a life. A real life.

I wanted him with every Alpha gene in my body. The bond that formed could not be ignored. It was a far too powerful force.

Even now, as he slept at my side while the darkness passed by all around us, I felt his presence edging my mind with an excruciating beauty and sense of wholeness. It felt as if I were reaching into a golden light which held all reasons for life itself to exist. If I didn't close my fist around that light, I'd lose it forever.

When we stopped for gas, I had Misha go into the bathroom and change into jeans and a t-shirt I'd bought him. I gave him a cologne that was made for Omegas, and hoped that would disguise his scent enough to fool anyone we might encounter on this journey. People would never assume a Sylph was wandering about in public anyway, but they might sense him as different, and I didn't want to bring any unwanted attention.

I figured the nurses at the colony would discover Misha's absence by seven a.m. when they woke him for breakfast and his shower. The way the media worked, we'd be news by noon.

Before noon I expected to be in Tarn and hidden away in the rental house I'd leased for the spring and summer.

Beyond that, with our new identities, and our new bond, I'd legally file us as an Alpha/Omega pair. After that, I'd worry about a job. I had enough money in cash to last us a year. And if Mathias came through with a loan on my house and, later, a sale, I'd have more.

I was young. The prospect of starting over did not deter me.

*

When we approached the border checkpoint, my nerves were strung taut. It was five minutes until seven. A half-dozen "what ifs" flooded my mind. If Misha was already discovered missing, they might have a police bulletin and recognize him even if it took hours to hit the media. Maybe the new I.D.s wouldn't pass inspection. Or they'd want to delay us for any number of reasons. Or maybe they simply wouldn't like how we looked.

The checkpoint was a glass cubicle. On both sides of the road were stop signs flashing red lights on top. A larger building stood off to the right of the checkpoint just ahead, on Tarn land. A large flood-light illuminated both constructs, and shone its bright glow across the road.

I slowed to a stop and rolled my window all the way down.

The strong light stung my eyes and I saw Misha tense.

As I came to a stop at the window and started to say, "Hello," the man inside glanced up. He had a paperback novel in his hand and looked at us with a dazed glare. Then without any expression, he casually waved us forward.

I thought for a second he was waving us to the side, but then I saw him turn away. He had waved us on. Given us the okay. And he had never asked for I.D. Sometimes it was that way in Tarn. It was stricter for people leaving the country than entering, not because of Tarn's laws, but because of high strictures enforced by other countries.

I took it as a good sign that Tarn was welcoming us. It would be right about now that the nurses would be discovering Misha's absence. We'd beat the clock.

Driving past the checkpoint, immediately the trees seemed taller, the air fresher, cooler. It was a north country, so the winters lasted longer.

I breathed in. It smelled like freedom.

"Do you smell it?" I asked Misha.

I saw his chest rise beneath the t-shirt as he took a deep breath. "What?"

"Your new kingdom."

In the dim light, I saw him flash me a smile so big it nearly eclipsed his face.

*

I drove on into the morning hours. I never felt tired. My body had relaxed a little, but I couldn't fully release my tension. I wouldn't feel safe until we pulled into the little tree-lined driveway of our new home.

The sun rose over the tops of the trees, turning the sky pale green and pink.

We had two more hours to go.

Misha sighed and moved sleepily against my side, waking.

"Are we close?" he asked.

"Yes." I put my hand on his head.

After a few minutes, Misha sat up, saying, "Being this long in a car makes my stomach feel funny. I've never ridden in a car before."

I cracked my window and cold air poured in. "Take deep breaths and look straight forward out the window. It will help you orient your brain."

Misha was silent for a minute.

"Let me know if you need me to stop."

"I won't be sick," he said quietly. "I promise."

159

"You don't have to promise something like that."

"I'm still a little scared of what might happen to us."

"I won't let anything happen to you. Do you believe me?"

He nodded hard.

When I finally pulled off the highway to the exit that would take us to the correct address, Misha was leaning forward to look out his side window, head moving back and forth. The light of the morning made everything look golden.

Two left turns and one tinier street later, I pulled into the driveway lined with pine trees.

"Your kingdom is beautiful," Misha said. "Whose house is this?"

"Ours."

He sat back. "I don't think it can be real."

I let out a nervous laugh. "I'm not sure, either."

"The bond is strong between us," he said. "But this is still so much so fast."

"There was no time. It was now or never. Never wasn't an option for me."

As I spoke, I realized I was shivering.

Misha blinked up at me with his wide, pure smile and everything was right again.

I parked the car in a cleared space behind the house. The nearest house was through the trees to the right.

"Let's get inside," I said when we stopped.

Misha opened the door and stepped out, his head tilting back to look at the blue morning sky overhead. When I came around the front of the car I saw him kneel and touch both palms to the dirt. He looked up at me.

"Geo." His eyes glistened. "Geo, it's too beautiful. It's like a dream. I don't want to wake up. Don't let me wake up."

I held out my hand.

He took it and stood, saying, "It's like I've been gone for many years and forgot, but now I'm home. My home. And you've been with me all along but I forgot that, too."

160

"I feel the same."

"When I played my games with you, I never dreamed it would lead to this. I wanted you. I wanted a bond, but I never really believed it would happen."

I squeezed his hand. "You didn't play any game. This was meant to be. I'm convinced."

"Geo, tell me it's not going to end." His voice broke on that last word and he stepped into my shadow and my arms.

I grasped him about the shoulders.

His arms came around my waist. He was almost as tall as I, muscular but thin, and I held him tight the way I had when I'd carried him to the bathing room, when I'd felt him become my responsibility, my charge. My Misha.

I'd fought it hard. But such barriers like guilt or the law did not work on mate-bonds. I hadn't realized we'd already started to form a bond that day in the baths. Not until I got the blood test. And even then, I'd gone into denial and demanded a second test.

Spiritual texts said the mate-bond was sacred and an Alpha separated from his Omega would shatter chains and break down walls to be with his intended. The Burn acted like a calling through the bond. An Omega responded much the same. He'd travel any distance or smash any door that kept him from his mate. Misha wasn't an Omega, but he was mine.

The philosophers were right. I'd done the impossible to get us to this point. I hadn't slept. I hadn't eaten. I'd relied on help from nefarious friends from my college years. I'd become a thief, a kidnapper, a criminal. I had focused only on getting Misha out of his incarceration and into my life, into my arms, and my heart.

I lowered my head and kissed his forehead. It was the second time I'd ever kissed him, and in nearly the same spot.

He lifted his head, his cheek grazing my jaw, his lips against my neck, my ear and then my own cheek. I only needed to turn my head an inch to cause our mouths to meet.

My lips brushed his and they were amazingly soft and silken, pliant and sweet. An expanding blaze of hunger rose inside me, but not for food. We were perfectly in synch; our mouths opened at the right moments, together, seeking more, wanting greater depth to our joining.

My cock pressed hard to Misha's own, throbbing so deeply it hurt.

Misha pulled back with a quick gasp. "Are you in the Burn?"

"My Burn has not come on yet. This is purely me wanting you."

"Well, I am in the Burn and I don't want to wait."

"I won't make you. As your mate, I am responsible for you. To take care of you forever. I'm yours." I realized my statements were almost like a marriage vow. I meant each and every word.

Misha smiled and then made a motion like a bow. "Your Grace, there is no greater gift than this."

He was so funny, so strange, so stunningly beautiful. I cupped his chin in my palm. I ran my fingers through his hair.

"Let's get inside." I turned toward the car. "Come here. I have a few bags of personal items in the car for us. We can unload the rest later."

Misha allowed me to load him up with several bags which included food, toiletries, and clothing. It was then I realized he was still barefoot.

"Oh hell."

"What?"

"You don't have shoes. I forgot shoes!"

He let out the sweetest laugh. Had I ever heard him laugh before? It was wonderful.

"You told me you'd have them for me," Misha said.

"I did. But I meant I'd buy them. We haven't had time yet."

"It's okay, Geo. I'm not going out right away. You can get them for me any time."

162

"It's just that I planned this so carefully. And you mentioned it and I didn't think. I thought I had everything."

Misha, laden with bags, stood looking at me. "My king. I would be shoeless and naked for you forever and be happy."

My face flushed. The unique Sylph energy of Misha accompanied those words. At this rate, I wouldn't last until we made it to the bedroom. With his constant Burn and Sylph pheromones, and my desire within our budding bond, I could barely think straight anymore.

I grabbed bags in both hands, elbowed the car door closed, and headed around to the front of the house and the porch.

It was a small house with an A-frame roof and pretty picture windows. The porch was small but contained an old dusty swing which made me think of my childhood. And of Mase. I would never forget him, but I was moving on now. He would be happy for me.

I set down my bags and fumbled in my pocket for my key. My cock was hard, the bulge in my pants proof of my aching desire. There was no turning back. I was consumed by my need and my affection—my love—for Misha. For it was love, even if it had happened at first sight. Love took what it wanted when it wanted.

When we entered the cabin, the air smelled a bit musty, but lemony. I'd had someone come and clean the place top to bottom, and make up the beds in the two bedrooms with new linens I'd bought.

When I'd made my short trip here and leased the house, I'd stocked the cupboards and refrigerator before I flew home.

The house was small but not claustrophobic. The ceiling rose up to a point in the living room, with strong wood beams against the rafters reflecting the yellow light from the windows.

The windows were wide with cheerful treatments in blue and purple. The place had come furnished, which was what I'd sought. I hadn't had the time to buy furniture, too.

Misha followed me inside, bare feet softly smacking the hardwood floor.

"Over here's the kitchen," I said, going to the open counter just past the living room and dumping the bags on top.

Misha came up beside me and set his bags alongside mine.

"Wow," he said. "This is great. I love it. I love it!"

Light shone in his eyes. "You did this for me."

I had done it for myself just as much. The bond made me feel pushy, greedy. But it also gave me an urgency to do anything for him. Give him all I could, whatever he wanted.

"This is your home now," I said. "And mine."

Chapter Nineteen

Misha

It was everything and too much at the same time.

What had Geo done?

When we'd pulled up to the house—our house—and I'd gotten out of the car, a cool breeze had blown into my curls, feathering them back. My skin remained hot, so that coolness was a big relief, almost as good as an orgasm.

I wasn't a child any longer. I knew there were no such things as knights in shining armor riding up on white horses to rescue virgin beauties. I knew the difference between fairy tales and reality. I'd told myself my fantasies so I could escape. So I could be free.

But then Geo came. King. Knight. Breaker of straight jackets and cuffs and locked doors. Rescuer of sane men who happened to be Sylphs.

And I believed in fairy tales again. Like a child.

I went from room to room, looking at everything in our new home. I touched every wall, every door frame and doorknob, all the countertop surfaces of the kitchen and bathrooms. Feeling it all, taking it all into me. I breathed in the clean scents. I looked at my ghostly and electric reflection in every window and every mirror, seeing a free man, a man in love.

Now that I had memorized the place, and left the oil of my fingertips over every surface, I wanted Geo so badly I couldn't wait.

I heard him in the kitchen putting away some of the things from the bags we'd carried in. Food and paper plates and napkins. Silverware and dishes. Towels. Tea bags in colorful square boxes.

I walked in the kitchen. "Which bedroom will be ours?"

Geo turned, his brown hair streaked with gold from the bright kitchen lights. "The one with the connected bathroom. It's called a master bedroom."

"Yes, that one is my favorite." I felt I should have known that little piece of information.

"Will you come there now?" I asked.

"Are you done exploring?"

"Yes. I love it all. I think it's an amazing castle." I smiled.

"Maybe more like a small keep." He chuckled.

We stopped talking, staring at each other now as if neither one of us knew who should make the first move.

I wanted him in my arms. I wanted him all over me, his skin and my skin, with no clothing. Naked and real. I knew it would feel overwhelming. Someone to touch for the first time. Someone to touch me in a way that was not medical, and without gloves. Someone who was safe. Who didn't fear me.

My stomach felt tied up tight and stabbed with flashes of intense heat at the same time. My skin flushed all over, a re-flush that went up and down my body at chaotic intervals. I wondered how my clothes kept from turning to ash.

Slowly, Geo raised his hand to me.

I raised mine. Our palms met.

"I can't wait," I whispered. I was a little scared again, my voice waning.

"You shouldn't have to anymore. Or ever again."

Mustering all my courage, I pulled him out of the kitchen and down the short hall to the biggest bedroom. The master bedroom, he'd called it. I had wanted that one for us. I had predicted he would, too, and I'd already turned down the covers.

I had searched the bedside drawers for sex aides but found none.

I wanted Geo from the moment I saw him. I'd never wanted anyone at the colony before, not like this. Only people in my imagination kissed, fondled and fucked me. Maybe it was

166

because I was programmed to know it was taboo. To know that I was somehow poison to the outside world.

When he let go of my hand and moved around the bed, I sat on the edge of the mattress. My guilt over everything that had happened kicked in large. Now was not the time for it, but I couldn't help it. My mind rushed with dark thoughts.

You are toxic.

You have caused upheaval and chaos that can never be fixed.

You are greedy, wanton, caring only for yourself.

You are everything the textbooks say about the evil madness of Sylphs.

How to stop the critical voice in the mind from undermining me? I hadn't figured that out yet.

I looked up as Geo—gorgeous Geo—leaned over me. In his hands were the very items I'd been searching the drawers for.

Lube. Two kinds. And towels. And another box that looked like wet-wipes.

He really had thought of everything.

My cock was so hard I probably could have pounded holes in the wall with it. The blue jeans I wore hurt and scraped the sensitive skin. I was used to loose jumpsuits, or all-out nudity in the safety of my own locked room.

I stood even as he waved me to stay seated.

"Geo, I--"

"Do you want a shower?" he asked softly.

It was probably a good idea. I'd walked bare-footed through dirt. I'd taken a long drive in a car feeling hot and bothered the whole time when I wasn't sleeping against Geo's shoulder.

And Geo, I decided, had to be tired. He had to be exhausted, actually, from everything he'd done.

He walked to the bathroom and said, "I'll turn on the hot water for you."

I heard the water go on, the splashing against the tile like a hard rain.

I entered the bathroom, still fully clothed. The small space was filling with luscious steam.

Geo stood by the shower stall, the door partially open. He stared at me as I entered.

"Geo," I started again. "I need to apologize to you."

"For what?"

"For making you do all this. For using my ways as a Sylph to make you want me just because I wanted you. You have to know I--"

"Hush," he said softly, placing one warm finger over my lips. "You didn't do anything I didn't want you to do."

"I did! I made you forget things, like gloves. I made you break protocols. I'm sorry. I'm so sorry I'm bad. I'm bad and I want all this, I do, but I don't deserve it."

"Misha, stop. Stop, sweetheart. I forgot my gloves on purpose just so I could feel you. Don't you know that?"

I shook my head. "I don't believe it. It's like with Tory, only you're nicer. Not violent. But it wasn't Tory's fault, either. I know that now. I'm bad and I make people want to do the wrong things. I know you will grow to hate me. I'm sure of it!"

More tears. Hadn't I cried enough already? But like my guilt, and my own poison soul, I couldn't help it.

"Shh." His arms came around me. "You're good and you have never done anything wrong. You're pure. I can feel it in my mind and heart. Our bond tells me this."

"But I enticed you. My body chemistry is what forced it, " I said.

"It wouldn't have formed if we weren't perfect for each other, true mates for each other. Don't you know that? This wasn't an accident. Bonds can't form without something like that to begin with, and certainly they need some sort of sexual contact. We've not even had that much. Knotting is the only way Alphas and Omegas fully bond. We haven't even gone that far and it's already strong. If nothing else, that is proof we should be together."

Now his hands were on my t-shirt at the hem, tugging, pulling it up. I raised my arms and let him sweep it over my head and off. His bare fingers touched me, sending swirling aches of pleasure throughout my burning body.

"This was meant to be, Misha. In history they used a term for us."

"What?" I croaked out.

"Fated mates. It's not really used anymore."

"But lust doesn't mean fated. It's just lust." I sniffed.

"No, it doesn't. But lust accompanies the feeling. The feeling is stronger. It is a knowing deep inside. It's like being drawn without your will, like a deep calling."

"I do feel that. Different from how I've ever felt before."

"Yes. And bonds are sacred. You fight them and you suffer. You ignore them but they don't go away that easily. I tried to will it away. It only got stronger."

"Me, too. I tried to block my feelings. I tried! I'm sorry, I'm so sorry!" I bumped my forehead against his shoulder.

"Stop this now. I didn't succeed in blocking you because I didn't want to succeed. I wanted you more than anything. And the bond itself knew. It's strong, very strong, and it will flourish no matter what."

Now Geo's fingers rested on the waistband of my jeans. Slowly, they undid the first button and slid the zipper downward.

My cock was pressed up against my belly and as soon as he parted the cloth it popped out, rigid and wet at the tip.

His hands pushed the jeans down my hips and they slid to puddle at my ankles. When I stepped out of them, I was fully naked before him, the shower raining behind him, the room humid with steam.

He ran his hands down my bare hips.

I wanted him to touch me, hold me, tease me, fuck me. I wanted everything with this Alpha man, this king, my so-honest and honorable chief of staff.

Instead of doing what I wanted right then, he gave me a little push, opening the shower door. "In," he said softly.

I stepped over the threshold and under the warm fall of water, my cock bobbing against my abdomen, my body heating and luxuriating as the water flowed over me. I ducked my head to get my hair wet and wash away my infernal tears.

I loved showers and baths. I had always wanted to take my time with them, but the nurses rushed me, never letting me linger. I tilted my head back and turned, allowing the warm water to pour fully over my hair.

I looked to the side and saw a little ledge holding soap, shampoo and conditioner. When I turned to reach for the soap, I heard the squeak of the shower door and felt the water against my back and side diminish.

A warm body pressed up against me from behind, arms going around my slippery waist. A large protrusion jutted up against my tailbone.

My heart stopped.

Geo's cock slid against me as he pulled me to him, the touch so intimate my vision went dark for a few seconds.

I almost came from that small contact, and combined with the knowledge of how much he wanted me, it made my thoughts spin.

My balance wavered, and it was as if my feet were not reliable anymore. I leaned back against him for support. Yes, for support, I told myself. It was all I could do.

His large hands clasped across my wet stomach, thumb edging my belly button, and I placed my own over his and turned my head. My wet hair streamed against his chest.

Slowly, I turned in his arms and we came face to face. My lips found his without me even trying, and he pressed forward, his tongue swiftly entering my mouth, licking, probing. I met his tongue with my own, deepening the kiss.

Our cocks met, skin to throbbing skin.

The water pounding our shoulders and backs seemed to cocoon us, erasing everything but who we were here and now,

170

each to the other. My guilt still stirred, but desire relegated to the back of the line. It would be dealt with another time.

Steam rose, thickening in my nose and throat. The kiss grew sweeter, harder. The Burn inside me forced me to want to take action. Now. But I held back. I'd practiced my entire adult life holding myself back, delaying my gratifications so I did not suffer injury.

But that practice did not take into account the pure ecstasy of being in Geo's arms. My mate. My bondmate.

I moaned into his mouth. My cock throbbed and again I thought I might come, but I managed not to. I felt every thrum of Geo's heartbeat, the pulse of it in his cock pushing up hard against my stomach.

I whined, leaning forward with my weight.

He pulled back. "Soon," he said.

He reached around me for the soap and began to lather my entire body.

I couldn't think anymore. I couldn't see or hear, but only feel.

I slumped against him as he washed me. It was what I had wanted in the bathtub back at the colony, his hands all over me. This and more. Never-ending.

After a few minutes, I rubbed my hands all over him, the soap suds between us combining, joining us in slick splendor.

I washed him and he washed me, though we fumbled a lot, all the blood in our systems pooled below, our cocks swollen beyond endurance.

I touched his buttocks, muscular and smooth, delving my fingertips neatly between his crack.

The water rinsed us constantly. My wet hair ran into my eyes.

Finally, Geo slid his hands down my belly and cupped my balls. I almost shot off right then and there.

He reached with his other hand and turned off the water. His hand left my crotch and he stepped out of the stall.

I followed. He grabbed a fluffy towel and turned, putting it over my head, blocking my sight. I heard him softly laugh as his fingers scrubbed the towel over my sopping wet hair.

I yanked the towel away and brought it to my chest.

He grabbed another towel and, as he back-walked out of the bathroom, he quickly skimmed it across his chest and thighs.

His cock bobbed as he threw his towel on the floor and fell back, sitting on the edge of the bed. He reached out with both hands.

I dropped my own towel, my skin still wet all over, and walked straight into his arms, standing between his legs and naked before him.

His hands went to my hips, gripping, and he held me in place, his head going down, his tongue coming out. He swiped it over the damp head of my jutting cock and I gasped. Without warning, he sucked the whole tip into his mouth.

Heat flared up all around me. I drew in a sharp breath and held it. All sensation and pleasure coursed to the head of my cock and I saw white.

"More!" I was suddenly out of control. I thrust, feeding more of my cock to him, and he took it.

I couldn't believe how good that suction felt. Like nothing my hand could ever mimic. Nothing my imagination could fully supply until I felt it, real and alive, right there, his mouth on me, his tongue, and the incredible bliss of that suction.

I put my hands on his shoulders and knocked Geo off balance. He didn't fight me but went onto his back easily as I knee-walked on the mattress up his body until I was straddling his chest. My cock rose up, my balls full and tight.

I reached forward and pulled my cock down toward his mouth again. His head was raised slightly, mouth open, and I fed it to him all the way to the hilt.

His eyes grew bright and he sucked and swallowed, taking me beautifully. I was afraid I'd choke him but he didn't choke. He moved his head back a little to breathe, then forward again to take me deep. I knew I was cutting off his air, but he sucked me hungrily and didn't push me away.

I felt my orgasm approaching. He must have, too, for he finally pushed me up and over until I fell hard on my back against the bed's pillows.

His hands went to my bent knees, shoving them open, and he lowered his mouth, his hand pulling my cock up from my belly, swallowing it once more, drinking it in all the way, then moving up and down on it until I heard myself yelling. My body rocked up and I came so hard that everything turned to falling stars and blackness.

My wet head tossed and turned on the soft pillows. I held my hand against my mouth to stop myself from screaming.

After my orgasm ended, Geo came up and pulled my hand away, his mouth going down on mine, opening, sharing the flavors of my ecstasy with me.

His hard cock pressed to my belly.

When he let up to breathe, I said, "Oh, that was--" I couldn't finish.

"Misha, Misha," he said, dropping kisses all over my face.

He held me close.

I couldn't believe how wonderful he was, how giving, how nurturing. I had never felt these things. I was overwhelmed. But not too much that I didn't know what I wanted. I wanted more.

I looked up at him. He was sparkling. I said, "I want you to put your cock in my mouth, too. Please."

His smile bloomed. "How you ask that question is just too sweet."

"I want it." My voice turned to a whine.

He came up over me. My head was slightly upturned, supported by the pillows. I opened my mouth as I saw his cock now bobbing before my face. It was big and thick, and glistening at the dark pink tip.

He took it by the base, so stiff and long and pretty, and fed it to me inch by inch. First I licked the head all over, delighting in the precum that dripped from the tip.

He threw his head back in pleasure.

Craving more, I sucked him in. Gently, he slid himself deeper. I opened wider, wanting it all, wanting to suck but worried about my teeth. Would I hurt him? I'd never done this before.

I placed my hands on his hips, caressing until I gripped his buttocks, and urged him on. I felt myself gag a little, but kept him pressed forward as it instantly passed.

I could do this! I was determined.

I bobbed my head, giving myself time to adjust with each movement. In. Out.

Geo let out a strangled moan and with his free hand slapped the wall over my head and leaned in.

I kept thinking over and over again that he was now mine. I had him in my grip. This naked man was over me, narrow hips flexing, moving, pressing into me, letting me bring him off to realms of pleasure.

He was so gorgeous kneeling over me. His skin was a bit browner than mine, and young and firm. The dark hair around his cock tickled my nose and cheeks. I was a supplicant to his power and I loved it. Perhaps he was right and he had enticed me as much as I had enticed him. Perhaps I wasn't a poisonous flower he'd bent down to caress. Or if I was a flower enticing him, then we both were, each to the other.

My arms were wrapped around his thighs, holding on tight as his hips thrust forward again and again. He was gentle but forceful at the same time. It made me think about control. I wanted to see him lose it altogether. I wanted to watch him break all his barriers and let go.

I sucked harder, tonguing him up and down his shaft. As he pulled out, I licked the head, diving my tongue into the crevice where his tiny hole was, never letting up.

He yelled only moments later, warning me in a gravelly voice. "I can't hold back!" He started to pull back, but I held him to me with my arms, lifting my head a little to take more of him in, and sucked hard.

His cock swelled and he cried out and let go, shooting strong, salty, tart streams of liquid down my throat. I swallowed fast, wanting it all. Wanting everything he had.

I loved it. This was Geo. Geo's essence and sacred self, and he was giving it to me. To me. I had made him feel this. I had made him scream.

When he managed to pull out, he was still dripping all over my lips and chin, rubbing the tip of his cock there.

My hands moved up and down his thighs, which shivered at my touch.

He backed off and fell to my side on his ass, his leg dragging over my knees. He curled against me and pulled me to him.

"Misha." As his hands brushed my face clean I opened my mouth and tried to lick them.

He leaned down and placed his mouth over mine and I was lost again. My cock arched toward my hip. The Burn never let up, but I had learned to ride it, instead of it riding me. For a moment, I could relax in my mate's arms.

We lay in each other's embrace for a while, caressing and kissing, until things heated up again for Geo. We moved against each other, learning what we liked, learning how our bodies responded.

"Will you knot me?" I asked, after we'd come again in each other's arms.

"I want to wait for the Burn. I want to do it with an intent toward a full bonding."

I thought of the lube he'd brought to the bed, and the towels. He'd come prepared, but now it seemed we both agreed. We would wait.

"I want nothing less than that if possible," I replied.

"We are making our own rules here." He spoke into my ear, his voice solid, his breath warm. "There is no guarantee. But if you respond like an Omega down there, and I knot you during the Burn, it will be complete."

"I don't know if I can wait. I want you now." I sounded almost petulant. Maybe I was.

Geo pulled me onto my side and wove his legs with mine. I rested my cheek on his chest, my forehead touching his chin. His outside arm wrapped around my waist.

Our bodies fit together in a comfortable and perfect union, hip to hip, rib to rib. I felt his soft cock against the inside of my thigh just above my knee and was careful not to press my weight in that area. My own cock throbbed with my heartbeat, half-hard, against the dip where leg met hip.

The day was bright outside, making the curtains of the bedroom glow. But with all of them drawn, it was dim and peaceful, soft gray shadows hovering on the walls.

I heard Geo's breathing become slow and even and knew he'd finally fallen to sleep. I wondered how long he'd gone without rest. Or food.

I moved my head up so I could gaze upon his face. Five o'clock shadow. Straight nose. Thick dark lashes against flushed cheeks. Bangs that scattered in curved clumps against his forehead. He looked young and pure, not like a kidnapper. Not like a man who'd lost his entire career.

His lips curved up slightly, a smile there as if he'd finally found the thing he'd been searching for his whole life.

Me.

Chapter Twenty

Geo

My Misha. I couldn't get enough of him.

I'd never had sex outside the Burn before. What I'd done with Mase had been a lot of fooling around, but never intercourse. Never real sex. Still, we'd formed a partial bond. It seemed I was good at that without even knowing it. Like it was a mysterious talent I had from some unknown source.

Sitting over me, Misha was exquisite, head thrown back, hard cock thrusting in and out of my mouth, hips rocking back and forth. He tasted sweeter than any Omega I'd ever had service me in the Burn. He rose up and down, his ass rubbing softly against my chest. He kept making sweet, strained noises of pleasure. He leaned over me, his sweet and feral Sylph scent increasing, his head down now, and looked me straight in the eye.

"Geo," he said.

My cock throbbed at the sound of my name spoken so reverently.

This was wrong. This was right. If ever caught, I'd possibly hang. Right now, I didn't care.

This was the second time he'd let me suck him in one day and I loved it. He enjoyed straddling me, being on top, pressing himself into my mouth. I didn't mind at all.

"I want this all the time with you. I never want this to stop."

He pulled out so I could take a breath and lick my lips. It gave me a chance to answer.

"Well, of course, you're a Sylph."

And I was an Alpha on the verge of the Burn. I had to admit, I never wanted it to stop, either, in or out of the Burn.

Tomorrow was the day on my calendar for my Burn to start. My cycle was regular and easy, usually lasting not more than two days. But I had a feeling it might last longer this time the way Misha made my body feel like it wanted to come apart and fly away into a million pieces, burning as they went.

*

Misha and I slept through most of the afternoon of our first day in our new home. By dusk I woke famished and put on a robe and wandered into the kitchen.

I found ingredients for chicken stir fry and whipped up a batch.

Misha must have been wakened by the aromatic promise of good food, for he joined me minutes later, clad in just his jeans, and we sat at the kitchen table by a small window and ate together, face to face.

His hair stood up in cute blond tufts from his forehead. It hung in wide ringlets at the base of his neck. So soft-looking, so pretty.

He looked relaxed and comfortable, casually chewing his food, when he suddenly blurted out, "I love you, Geo."

My vision misted.

"I love you, too. My Misha." There. I'd finally stated it aloud. It felt like another huge release, one that was necessary even after all our lovemaking and napping together. The words were out there now and could not be pulled back, undone, unsaid.

His smile went wide.

I leaned toward him and we kissed over the table, our food forgotten for a moment.

When we pulled back, Misha was glowing, his smile huge. He lifted his fork and began again to eat, but his eyes never left mine.

We finished eating and took our plates to the sink. I rinsed them while he marveled at the dishwasher, a thing he'd never seen before, along with most appliances in the kitchen.

178

After the kitchen was clean, we looked at each other and said in unison, "Back to bed."

He hopped forward and practically ran to the bedroom. I entered just in time to see him throw himself onto the mattress with its wrinkled covers, and bounce once on his side.

I wasted no time following him, throwing off my robe and straddling him with my hands and knees. Soon I was undoing the clasp of his pants and tugging them away to reveal his body to me once again.

I couldn't get enough.

*

I stood by the plate glass windows leading to the small, fenced yard and pressed my forehead against the glass.

Morning had come and true to my very rigid cycle, the Burn was coming upon me. It didn't care that I'd had enough sex yesterday to wear myself out. A fever crashed into my brain and mind, coursing through my body like waves of a hot sea.

Misha walked up to me and put a hand on my shoulder.

Even though I knew he was there, it startled me, and I turned abruptly.

"I can feel you," he said. "In here." He tapped the side of his head.

"I'm sorry."

"Why? It's just the Burn. I feel it all the time. It's wonderful."

"I know, it's just I feel—guilty."

For a moment, Misha looked stricken. "Are you upset? I hope not. My burden should never have been yours and now it is."

Both my hands rose and I framed his face with them, stroking his cheeks. "You have never been a burden. I'm the bad guy here."

"What?" He let out a short laugh.

"I took you. I've bound you to me now. I broke protocols, rules and laws all set into place for a reason. I'm an Alpha and I'm supposed to protect those around me. Those protocols and laws are to protect you. I failed."

He let out a huff of air. "You have *not.*"

"I've brought you from one captivity to another. Taken you to a place of further dependency and few rights even with your new identity as an Omega. What kind of a life have I led you to? How could I have been so selfish?"

My mind went manic sometimes in the Burn. But I'd been that way all week, so I couldn't tell if the Burn made it worse or if I was simply having a fit of conscience.

"Why do you think these things?" Misha asked. "I'm away from the castle that kept me trapped under its curse for twenty years. You risked your life for me. You lost your career for me. You gave me your entire being. I've never imagined a greater gift could be given to me. For the first time in my life I'm not alone. For the first time I feel whole." He gripped my forearms hard. "If I could have that for only one day, it would be worth everything. Except your own safety and happiness. For that, *I'm* sorry. *I'm* the bad guy."

"No," I started to argue.

"I'm the one who has wronged *you*," he continued. "I seduced you to me and you've lost everything. For what? For me? I'm nothing. I know I'm not a real prince. I only told myself these things to comfort away my fears and despair. What you have done for me, risked everything, is too much. I'm not a victim here. I've destroyed my king."

Tears rolled down his face and I wiped them away with my thumbs. "No, no," I began.

"And I can never give you children," he added in a small, forlorn voice.

"Hey," I said. The Burn flared, but gently, as if to encompass us both. "Listen to me. If we ever want them, we can use a surrogate."

180

Misha inhaled sharply. "I never thought about having children. Not ever, until now. But—but I wouldn't ever want to see you with someone else. I can't stand the thought."

"Neither can I," I replied. "It can be done in a lab. We don't even have to meet the birth-father. We never have to see or know him. It can be done."

"It can?"

I nodded. "Easily. Some day. When we're ready."

"I'd love children from you," Misha said. He put his palm against my chest as if feeling for my heartbeat. "With all my heart."

My Burn liked his answer. It flickered inside me. My cock rose hard and strong as it began to take over my body and rule with the mating urge. "Some day, then."

Almost a whisper, "I can feel you." Misha smiled at me. "Your Burn. It's a different feeling from my own. Like the ocean crashing against the beach. It's beautiful. Will you knot me? Make me yours finally? I feel like I've been waiting for you my whole life."

I nodded, still holding back for some reason. If the Burn had its way, I'd be ravaging Misha on the floor right now. Instead, I said as calmly as I could, "Let's go make this bond permanent."

Hand in hand we entered our bedroom.

*

Our first morning home. And I was in the Burn.

Earlier, Misha had risen, smiling, and opened all the curtains, letting in the light and the greenness of the land.

Now, as we came into our new shared room, he let go of my hand and went to the windows, beginning to shut the drapes.

I wanted some light. More than gray shadows. Usually, with Omegas from Zilly's chattel farm, I didn't care if it was night or day, dark or light. With Misha, I wanted to glory in him. I wanted to see him in the golden day. We were hiding and would have to keep secret who he really was for the rest of our lives, but in the bedroom I did not want us to hide.

I pointed toward the largest window over a spread of low, empty shelves. "Keep that one open."

He turned toward me, then glanced alongside me to the bed. "The light makes dappled patterns on the blankets," he said. "I like it."

Suddenly, I felt dizzy. I had to sit. My knees bent and I nearly collapsed on the side of the bed.

Misha moved quickly, standing before me, his blond hair a little wild, his heart-shaped face and pale blue eyes intent on me.

"You need to knot me." His voice was breathless, but calm. His boldness charming.

With two of us in the Burn together, I wondered, if we'd set the room on fire.

Before yesterday, Misha was a virgin in every way. Technically, he still was. He'd never been touched like this before. The Burn might make him want it, and it might spiral me into unchecked desire, but we both needed to do all we could to take it slow for our first time.

My cock throbbed. It didn't want to go slowly at all. It wanted to plunge into Misha's willing body and let loose until I couldn't breathe. I knew it might hurt him. He didn't know that. Though he had the most control in this moment, I had to take charge as best I could. He'd suffer for me and never say a word. I could tell by his eagerness, and his sweet nature.

"We need to put some rules into place."

"Rules? Do we need them? We can already sense each other, feel each other," he said.

His hand on my shoulder tightened. I responded by reaching for him.

He pushed me back onto the bed and straddled me with his still-clothed body. Only a stray pair of jeans, and a simple t-shirt covered him, but he looked good in them. The jeans cupped his ass in firm support.

My hands went there instantly, clutching his buttocks through the rough, thick material.

"Misha, I want you badly but it can't happen until you're prepared."

"I *am* prepared."

Just hearing him say those words sent flashes of heat through my body.

"Not quite. You aren't an Omega. You need to be stretched and lubed."

He was quiet for a moment.

"Won't I just get used to you in me after a while?"

So innocent. My blood nearly boiled. "You would, but I don't want that. I want it comfortable for you. Good for you."

"Do you have enough control to wait?" He glanced off toward the shower.

"I don't mean you need to prepare yourself. You need to let me. If I can keep it together. I want to give you pleasure. So there will be no hesitation between us."

"You're in the Burn. You need to knot now."

"So are you. And there are a lot of things to give us both pleasure until you're ready. My Burn makes me want all of it."

"You still have control, then," Misha said.

"Yes." I hadn't lost myself completely. I shoved him over my side and onto his back. He didn't fight and raised his arms willingly as I pulled off his shirt.

Next came his jeans. I slid them down his long legs and threw them so hard across the room they hit the wall.

His skin was a pink-gold all over, flushed, and his cock bobbed up in eagerness for me. I dipped my head and ran my tongue down the underside of the shaft and he quivered. So lovely. I had to keep reminding myself of my own words spoken moments ago. He wasn't a ready Omega. Yet I wanted to push his legs open and back. I wanted to thrust into him.

He was so pretty, glints of blond hair framing his cock, the faint glitter of it brushing his tight, round pink balls.

I pushed my hands underneath him and lifted him a little. His knees bent. His legs spread.

"Do what you want to me," Misha said, sighing, lifting himself. "Do whatever you want."

Consent. Was it even possible between two madmen in the midst of their Burns?

I pulled my hands forward and clasped the globes of his ass, spreading as he pulled his knees up closer to his body.

His tiny, virgin pink bud greeted me, framed by more short golden hair, and I'd never desired anything more in my life. It was waiting. Had been waiting years. For me.

I ran my tongue along his crack and circled the dent, the entrance.

Misha began to cry out, nonsense words with long vowels. Oh. I. Ahhhh.

I loved that tune.

I used my tongue to wet him more, my cock pulsing with need, urging me to hurry. I coated him with my saliva, loving the essence of him, relishing in this act of love toward my mate.

Even after this short amount of time, it was love. I could feel the white hot light of it in our existing bond.

With my mouth, I felt him shiver a little, the muscle of the aperture moving in pleasure, constricting but also loosening as I pushed with the strong muscle of my tongue, licking harder, finally breaching.

I pushed my tongue in and out of him and heard him yell.

I let him dangle on the precipice of bliss for another minute before pulling away, lifting my head.

"I need to stretch you."

He handed me the lube. He had been ready with it in his hand. I almost laughed. We were both in such a hurry but we needed to take our time.

I was not conservative with the lube. No need. I poured a large amount onto my hand and slicked him up. I poured more on my fingers, then massaging his opening until I felt I could deftly and painlessly slide one finger in.

"Oh, that's good," he yelled. "It's good. Can you knot me now?"

So eager. I loved it. No Omega had ever spoken to me like that.

My cock was large enough that one finger was not enough of a stretch.

"Just a little longer, okay?"

"Yes, Your Grace."

I chuckled. Did we still have enough sanity and control for humor? I loved it.

I took out my finger and poured more lube on my hand.

This time, I breached him with two fingers, going slowly, massaging as I went.

"Geo, that's a lot. That feels so full."

I was bigger than two fingers. He'd soon feel fuller.

"Patience." I didn't know if I said the word for myself or for him. For I was using all my will power to hold back from fucking him from one second to the next.

"I want you in me. Now," he demanded.

Three fingers would stretch him well, but for a moment he'd be uncomfortable. I couldn't bear it. I looked down at him, so hard, so flushed and willing. His cock bobbed against his stomach, dripping at the head.

Just as I introduced a third finger, I leaned down and with my free hand pulled his cock straight up and sucked the tip into my mouth.

Misha wailed. Opened. Thrust up and deeper into my mouth while impaling himself on my fingers.

I sucked him hard and he yelled my name.

With my middle finger, I searched and wiggled inside him until I found his prostate. In Omegas, their insides were lined with pleasure points all the way into the rectum and

185

toward the mouth of the uterus. The inner chamber secreted natural lubrication, though often not enough. Even they needed external lube to help keep them slick and ready, especially for an Alpha in the Burn who might use them for days before cooling and calming.

Sylphs were like Omegas in that they didn't knot. But they were more like Alphas without the extra slick or pleasure points. But pleasure could still be found. We all had prostates, testicles and penises, each and every gender of our race.

When I found the gland inside him and stroked, Misha's cock throbbed in my mouth.

I pulled off quickly. I didn't want him to come until I was fully inside. We needed to cement the bond. I needed to knot him and he needed it to feel like the best thing in the world.

"Geo, please. Your Grace, I beg you! I want you inside me. I want you to knot me. I can't wait any more!"

There was no more holding back. I dared anyone to say they could in this situation. I was in the first throes of my Burn. He was ready, he was burning, and he was begging.

He pulled his legs back against his chest, offering himself. "Please," he said over and over. "Please."

I removed my fingers and quickly poured lube onto my aching cock. I did the best I could without touching it, without friction. I was so close to coming.

I positioned myself on my knees between his legs. He was open for me, his entrance glistening and ready, no longer the tight little bud, but stretched now, round and open, beckoning.

I took hold of my cock at the base, rubbed the tip up and down his crack once, then plunged within. I wanted to take it slow, and I tried. I barely stopped myself from going to the hilt and stayed still half way in as Misha, beneath me, gasped for air.

Sweat dripped from my brow.

He didn't cry out. He didn't make a sound. For long seconds we were frozen. His insides were scorching and tight against my stiff cock. It felt good. Too good. I wanted to move. But I waited.

I could feel him in my mind assessing it all. His body adapting. His emotions overflowing with white-winged rapture.

I wanted to give him the world and everything in it. I couldn't do that at the moment. But I could give him this.

Together we made the decision. As my control broke and I could hold back no longer, he thrust up, impaling me all the way.

My balls slapped his crack. I was in. Inside my Misha.

"Oh, Geo, you're so big. Is it in? Is it all the way? Push."

"It's in, my love."

"Move," he ordered.

I responded instantly, pulling out half way and pushing back in. He stuttered and gasped. He had lost his voice. Only a keen came from him now.

I pulled out again, nearly all the way this time, then pushed in harder.

"Do it faster," he ordered. "Knot me!"

My sweet virgin knew what he wanted.

I would knot this time for sure. It wasn't going to last. I could already feel my orgasm rising through me, gathering at my lower back and my balls and pushing forward.

I pistoned my hips now, almost ruthless, his lubed passage opening even more for me, a perfect fit. His muscles squeezed my cock until I saw stars.

With every breath he exhaled, he made loud moans and gasps. He reached up and grabbed my shoulders, using the leverage to sit up and wrap his arms more tightly about my upper back.

I leaned into the embrace, reaching up from the center of our joining and putting my arms up under his shoulders to pull him to me. Embracing tightly, the bond grew in my mind like a blooming flower as I pumped my hips.

It was incredible. A fever ran over my skin. Every part of me tingled. I mated him hard and fast in those last few seconds until everything exploded and my cock pulsed with one huge throb and I shot inside him.

I hadn't ever known such a high. I'd knotted Omegas before, and it was good, but this was above and beyond anything I'd ever known.

Misha was with me, coming between us, the hot liquid helping to seal us together into a single entity.

I felt my knot grow fast at the base of my cock and pushed harder to lock us together. It formed faster than I'd ever experienced, sending me reeling into greater ecstasy.

Beneath me, Misha jutted his hips up and groaned. Our lips were joined, our tongues meeting. I hadn't remembered how we came to be kissing, but the contact made me want him even more.

How could there be more than this?

My cock pulsed. Opening my eyes just a crack, I saw the room spinning, and closed them fast. I let myself sink into Misha as he clung to me, as we fought to breathe, to stay together, and to merge into one.

I felt Misha's legs fold around my back, his heels sliding down a little to dig into my buttocks.

I turned my head reluctantly away for breath. I needed oxygen, and so did he, but we were back to kissing in seconds.

My cock throbbed and shot off again as I felt my knot move. It was so much pleasure I thought I would die. Usually, I had some reprieve. The knot would form, I'd stay joined to my Omega sex partner, and not come again until it reached to just below the head of my cock and start to pulse.

But now I filled Misha up even more, and the knot kept moving and growing and pulsing, the liquid flowing from the head of my cock.

He moaned, tearing his lips away from mine, tossing his head.

I held him close to my chest. In my mind, I held him even closer. I could feel him, my Sylph lover, like a wave of happiness skipping about my thoughts.

This beautiful man was mine. I'd lost everything to save him. I'd lost nothing that mattered, though, for he was everything to me, and I had time.

For now, we were the universe coming together in a huge, convulsive quake of pleasure.

My knot tickled and teased me as it moved up to the tender head of my cock. Then the rapid pulsings started again, and I shot hard inside him and didn't let up.

Misha's cock throbbed where it was trapped between us. He came at again, a gush of heat against my stomach and chest.

I lost all sense of balance and buried my head between his shoulder and chin, pressing down.

Everything was flashing light and darkness. Then nothing.

I woke to hands combing through my hair, and soft but garbled words. I could make out nothing but my name spoken over and over.

"Misha," I replied, my breath heavy on his ear.

"You're awake," came the whispering reply.

We were still joined. Slowly, I pulled out of him, careful of his sensitivity after such a mating. The incredible amount of liquid I had ejaculated made the passage smooth and easy. I slid out and realized we need a towel right away.

I had set a stack by the bed yesterday and reached over to grab one, balling it up between Misha's legs.

His long, lean body lolled beneath me, head back on the pillow, eyes half-closed.

"How do you feel?"

"Geo," he said. "That was—that was beyond amazing. You were in my mind. I felt you like a—like a sparkling force of light, like lightning. Like a storm over the sea. I want more. More."

The fires of my Burn had banked a little right now. I could think again. It wouldn't last.

"I want more, too," I said, smiling down at him.

"When can we do it again?" The question was asked with such a pure, innocent need that my depleted cock jumped in response.

"Very soon," I replied. "And all day if you wish."

"I wish," he said. "I wish I wish I wish."

He would get that wish and more. In my Burn it would happen over and over. And his Burn made him constantly want it.

It was going to be a fantastic next couple of days.

Epilog

Misha

I rested in the plush chair by the window, looking out over the small realm of our tiny keep.

If there had ever been others like me, who had escaped and bonded to wonderful Alpha mates, they wouldn't be written about, they wouldn't be known. It was illegal. They would be in hiding. Myths and rumors.

I was fully engulfed in the Burn, still and always, but more content than I could ever remember feeling because I had been mated. Geo had mated me. Knotted me. My world had transformed. I'd never known such peace.

Tingling and hot, but full and unafraid, the tension in my body I'd felt my whole life was gone.

My king came into the room and my gaze turned away from the forest and fields and onto him. I couldn't look away. He was beautiful. He was mine.

He had come to my castle where I'd been locked up, a prince awaiting his birthright. Waiting to come of age. He'd freed me and shown me his soul, and we were still exploring it. I hoped we always would be.

I was hungry for him, for the whole wide world, everything he'd gifted to me.

Our new realm waited. Me as his mate, Omega to the outside world, Sylph in our private deeds.

"Misha," he said softly, drawing me with his voice.

"Your Grace," I replied, getting up and going to him, putting my arms around him, pressing up against him to feel his need.

He was ready for me. Always ready to give me anything I wanted.

For I was his devoted prince and he was my king, forever without end.

This was the story I told myself, but it was no longer an escapist fantasy taking me away from a dry, gray world. It was a true story now.

And it was mine.

THE END

Contact links for Wendy Rathbone:

Join my Facebook group Wendyland. I post updates, cover reveals, snippets, sales and other fun stuff every day:
https://www.facebook.com/groups/718074255203918/

Friend me on Facebook:
https://www.facebook.com/wendy.rathbone.3

Follow my Amazon author page:
https://www.amazon.com/Wendy-Rathbone/e/B00B0O9BMS/ref=dp_byline_cont_ebooks_1

Follow me on Bookbub:
https://www.bookbub.com/authors/wendy-rathbone

Dear Reader:

Thank you for reading *Alpha's Embrace: The Omega Misfits Book 3.*

I so loved inventing a new gender for my omegaverse: Sylphs. Misha is very close to my heart. I hope to give him a cameo in a future book in this series. Every part of this book's process toward publishing was a joy!

Next on my agenda is book 4 in *The Omega Misfits* series: *Single Omega Dad.* I hope you come along with me on this journey of continuing my discovery of this wonderful genre.

Happy Reading!

Love,
Wendy Rathbone

About Wendy Rathbone

Read Wendy Rathbone… where imposters and outcasts, princes and lost boys always find their happily every after.

I have written in all genres: sci-fi, fantasy, horror, paranormal, contemporary, erotica, romance. But I keep coming back to romance as the main focus. Gay romance. Male/male romance. The idea of two men falling in love is irresistible to me. It's all I write now.

All my books are available on Amazon and most are in Kindle Unlimited. So if you have the urge, go take a look. See what's on the shelf.

Male/male romance books by Wendy:

The Kingdom of Slaves Series (contemporary fantasy mm romance)

The Slave Palace
The Slave Harem
Master of Halloween (short story)

The Omega Misfits (Omegaverse mm romance)

Trust No Alpha
The Alpha's Fake Mate
Alpha's Embrace
Single Omega Dad (coming May 2020, Mathias's story!)

The Imposter Series (fantasy mm romance)

The Imposter Prince
The Imposter King

The Moonling Prince Series (fantasy, sci fi mm romance)

The Moonling Prince
The Coming of the Light

The Foundling Series (contemporary billionaire mm romance trilogy)

Rescue Me
Sacrifice Me
Remember Me

The Fantastic Immortals Series (fantasy/myth mm romance)

Ganymede: Abducted by the Gods
Zeus: Conquering his Heart

Stand Alone Novels

Sci Fi MM Romance

Solstice Gift (holiday)
Not Another Hero
Cocky Virgin Prince
Prey
Scoundrel
The Android and the Thief (Second edition coming May 2020)
Letters to an Android

Fantasy MM Romance

Lord Vampyre
Lace
Snow of the White Hills (mm fairy tale)
The Elves of Christmas (holiday fantasy mm romance)

Contemporary MM Romance

Romantically Incorrect
Snowfall and Romance (Christmas novel)
The Bodyguard's Valentine
Buying You

TRUST NO ALPHA
Wendy Rathbone

It's a world gone mad. The Alphas are out of control.

When you discover you're not who you thought you were, the nightmare begins.

KRIS

At age eighteen, life as he knows it is over for Kris. A secret to his nature he was not aware of has been revealed.

Now, kept as a prisoner in a locked room in the mansion of his wealthy father, Kris is at the mercy of Alpha laws and Alpha domination.

Things take a turn for the worse when his own litter mate threatens him, and his father starts behaving strangely around him.

Escape is his only hope. But where can he go in a world that allows him no rights?

THORNE

Marked as a dangerous Alpha, and living a secluded life alone and unloved, Thorne still grieves for the mate whose death he feels responsible for.

Years have passed, and he refuses to even try to function in normal society.

One day he discovers a young man on his property, disheveled, desperate, and scared. He acts like a runaway Omega, but he doesn't smell like one.

What is this boy? And why does Thorne feel an immediate need to protect him? To bond him? To make him his?

A non-shifter, Omegaverse love story of rescue, first time, fertility issues and an HEA. Standalone read. 65,500 words. (While Omegas are birth-fathers in this universe, there is no on-page mpreg in this book.)

THE ALPHA'S FAKE MATE
Wendy Rathbone

The Alphas think they own everything. Including people. Well, I'm here to say they don't own me, and I will never let one of those bastards touch me again.

The frenzy of their Burn cannot be trusted. I know from experience. My first time with an Alpha nearly ended in my death. And because of the laws which favor Alpha rights, and place a large number of unbonded, adult Omegas on chattel farms, my abuser can never be tried for his crimes against me.

Omegas are being hurt. Omegas are dying.

All Alphas are violent. Or so I believe. Until I meet Orion.

Ori is everything a guy could want in a mate. Six foot three. Beautiful brown wavy hair. Bright, dark eyes. Muscles like chiseled marble. He even says "please" and "thank you" at all the right times. He's got it all, except he's an Alpha.

Though he has given me a room in his home free of charge, and has signed fake paperwork saying we are bonded so I don't have to answer my attacker's claim, can I trust him?

But now I'm in danger. If I don't take a real mate, my life as I know it will be over. Can I believe in the goodness of Ori? Can I learn to love again?

A non-shifter, fake mate, Alpha/Omega love story. Rescue. First time. Omegaverse. Mpreg. Healing from sexual trauma. (All books in The Omega Misfits series are standalone reads and can be read in any order.) 61k words.

SNOWFALL AND ROMANCE
Wendy Rathbone

A blizzard. A Christmas rescue. A man with the heart of an angel.

Hayden
Hayden knows it was stupid to think he could walk home from the office and beat the blizzard. So what if he worked out all the time until he was big and strong. So what if he hated to ever ask for help. Loners who think they can do everything themselves are just as vulnerable as anyone. His only consolation is if he dies there will be very few people who will miss him.

Matthew
The half-frozen man falling through the door to Matthew's coffee shop is more than alarming, but it's a good thing he'd forgotten to lock that front entrance or the beautiful guy covered in snow might have died in the cold.

The man is gorgeous, soft-spoken, helpful, maybe even a bit old-fashioned in his manners. Just the type Matthew always wished for but never met. Sharing a fire and a snowed-in night with him will be no hardship.

When the storm lasts more than a day, attraction blooms. But when it is over, will Hayden and Matthew's feelings fade? Or will holiday charm and a heart-warming miracle draw them together again?

Rescue, forced proximity, overwhelming attraction, blizzards, and a heart-warming Christmas miracle.

Although this book is part of A Snow Globe Christmas series, it is a complete stand alone and it isn't a requirement that you read the previous books to follow along. We wish everyone a happy holiday season.

THE SLAVE HAREM
Wendy Rathbone

The slave harem is all. If you enter, you can never leave. Contact with the outside world is forbidden.

With a secret talent for seeing auras of physical and emotional arousal, Ren, a sought-after pleasure slave, is sold to a mysterious master in a foreign land where he will become part of a collection of beautiful men.

Though the men appear welcoming, there is competition and jealousy among the ranks. And their mysterious master who is heard but never seen elicits more questions than answers.

One friendly slave, Li Po, helps Ren settle in, but it is the voiceless man, Zanti, who draws Ren's attention. With his wicked beauty and bratty scowls, Zanti is the least welcoming of them all, and Ren's training and control are put to the test.

Gay harem, slow-burn, enemies to lovers. Extraordinary and strange. Hot and cold. This book explores the many levels of sex, lust, loneliness and belonging. And maybe, just maybe, there can be love.

THE SLAVE PALACE
Wulf and Locke
WENDY RATHBONE

Conquered. Captured. Sold as a pleasure slave.

After being taken as a prisoner of war, Wulf fights his captors and is sold as a One-Night Thrall to be used and abused, then put to death. He is purchased by a high ranking master of the famous Slave Palace. Why Locke buys him, Wulf has no clue, but something about this master is intriguing. Instead of abuse, Wulf is plied with luxuries he has never known by a man who actually seems to respect him.

Jaded. Looking for a challenge.

Eminent Master Locke takes on a bet with his best friend that he can't train and tame a dangerous One-Night Thrall in ten days. But something about this slave stirs him like no other before. All bets aside, Locke has the urge to keep Wulf, as well as save his life. But Wulf is fierce, unwilling, and his consent papers have been forged. If Wulf doesn't soon submit to his role as a slave, he will be sent to death as a prisoner of war.

A sweet, slow-burn love story taking place on an alternate contemporary Earth where owning pleasure slaves is legal.

LORD VAMPYRE
Wendy Rathbone

When Lord Neverelle becomes a guest at Cliffside Keep, Vanni watches helplessly as Damion, the young man he's grown up with and secretly loves, falls for the alluring and seductive stranger. Lord Neverelle is danger incarnate, and soon takes control of the household.

Not satisfied with Damion alone, Never uses a vampire trick called "the tempt" to compel Vanni, who is swept into a love triangle that includes fiery passion and nightly threesomes.

Now Vanni must ask himself, is any of this consensual? And what about Damion—does he really want to be with Vanni, or is it all a sensual play controlled by vampire compulsion?

M/M and M/M/M romance.

The Imposter Prince
Book 1 in The Imposter Series
Wendy Rathbone

His love for an enemy prince threatens his very life.

Dare does not mind serving the spoiled and cruel Prince Darius. Growing up with him, Dare does everything for Darius including homework, bed play demands, and even doubling for him as the prince grows too paranoid to face even the smallest of crowds.

But everything changes in a single moment when Dare, while posing as Darius, is abducted by the enemy.

A captive in a new and hostile land, Dare meets another prince who seems just as indulged and rotten as Darius—until Dare gets to know him, until they fall in love. Against his will, Dare must continue to play the role of Prince Darius for real, or risk everything: his love, his land, and his very life.

His only chance for survival is to keep a secret from the one he loves, a secret that is also killing him.

A male/male, enemies to lovers novel of mad kings, troubled princes, abduction, fevers, cold dungeons, warm hearths, comfort, wine, and true love.

BUYING YOU
Wendy Rathbone

It's one thing to be a beautiful cover model on billboards, buses and magazine covers. It's quite another to be sold as one.

Prized for his looks, Dane knows it's shallow, but he is on his way to having it all. It feels good to be gorgeous, smart and have top designers from around the world requesting him.

When he returns to his hometown to participate in a small Date-For-Charity auction, it seems harmless enough—until a hooded man walks in and bids higher on him than anyone else. Dane is intrigued but nervous when he finds out the guy has vanished after the winning bid, leaving only a limo behind to whisk Dane off into the night.

Enemies to lovers, opposites attract, and hot steamy nights that challenge two guys' trust issues along with their biggest fears.

The Foundling, Rescue Me (Book 1)

What do you do when you find an unconscious man floating on a raft in the middle of the Caribbean? Rescue and fall in love with him, of course!

Well, that's not me! I'm a businessman first and foremost with an underworld reach that stretches from my island all the way to Miami. I'm too busy to rescue strays. I have no time for lovers. And I don't fall in love.

But Alec is beautiful, vulnerable, and my heart won't stop pounding. My every waking thought is of him. I can't concentrate. The world is suddenly vibrant and colorful. Flowers assault me with their sweet fragrance. Food tastes fresher. And my body is hot, so hot all the time.

I have done some dark deeds in my life and cared little for their affects on others as long as they gained me everything I sought. But now… one good deed and I don't know who I am anymore.

Billionaire, organized crime, amnesia, hurt/comfort, tropical hot-hot, happy for now. Book one of the Foundling trilogy. (Previously published under the title "The Foundling," this book is a newly edited, updated edition.)

The Foundling, Sacrifice Me (Book 2)

What do you do when your beautiful new lover's life is in danger and he wants to be bait to catch the enemy? You protect him with all your might.

Alec is still trying to remember who he is and is haunted by terrible nightmares. Diego is being investigated for murder. Their chemistry grows hotter and stronger even as Diego's ex, Sasha, comes for a visit and looking for a job.

Who can they trust to help them? Enemies are everywhere and the jungle closes in.

The Foundling, Remember Me (Book 3)

What do you do when your memories return and the most horrific nightmare you can imagine is real?

You try to bury it. You try to run. But none of that works.

Your lover is rock solid. He is always there for you, but is it enough?

Diego and Alec now live under witsec in San Francisco, thousands of miles away from the Caribbean. But their past still haunts them.

Alec is beginning to remember who he really is, but reliving the torment he went through threatens to destroy his sanity. Is Diego's love enough to hold onto such a broken man?

SONS OF NEVERLAND
A Deliciously Dark Male/Male Romance
Della Van Hise

Set against a backdrop of contemporary culture, *Sons of Neverland* explores the universal questions of love, sex and death - the three most crucial challenges every human being must face. Stefan London is a grieving man, suffering through the loss of his young daughter. When he goes to a science fiction convention in the hopes of meeting her friends, he encounters instead a man who is dangerously seductive. Lured into the night, Stefan soon discovers himself in a world where vampires are real, and immortality is only a kiss away.

But the price of eternal life is high, and as his handsome maker warns, "Through my blood you will learn a secret that will compel you to live forever, yet a secret so sinister it will haunt you for that same eternity."

The secret will haunt you, too.

***

One Reviewer said...
"Sons of Neverland" brings the reader face to face with the possibility that nothing we have been told by teachers, peers and priests holds a single gram of truth. The book is told in the poetic voice of myth, from the perspective of a man devastated by grief. As the story unfolds, Stefan's faith is not only tested, but destroyed - leaving him devastated but simultaneously free for the first time in his life... daring to stare love in the face of an immortal vampire."

YEAR OF THE RAM
Della Van Hise

Year of the Ram was described by one reviewer as... "A space-faring gay romance full of love, angst, and longing."

Only after Star Commander Morgan Diego becomes an exile as a result of a Galaxy Corps political blunder does he begin to realize how much he valued the companionship of his second in command - the mysterious Lucien, an Alfarian who is more elfen than human, with peculiar powers & abilities which begin to unfold as he, too, realizes what he has lost.

Separated by circumstance from his former life, Morgan is thrust into a world where he must survive by his wits. When he meets a peculiar little old man calling himself Kim Le, Morgan finds himself in a situation where he is required to master The Art - not only a form of human & extraterrestrial martial arts, but a way of living that will alter his life forever.

At the temple, he is introduced to his new teacher, another Alfarian man who begins to steal his heart - a heart which is already promised to Lucien. Torn and conflicted, Morgan struggles with the world he left behind and the world he now inhabits.

Beginning to believe he may never again return to his ship and to the friends and loved ones he left behind, he is all the more frustrated and heartbroken when a new Master arrives at the temple: a man to whom Morgan is immediately drawn both mentally and physically, a man who is strikingly familiar... yet utterly alien.

Eye Scry Publications

www.eyescrypublications.com

www.ingramcontent.com/pod-product-compliance
Lightning Source LLC
Chambersburg PA
CBHW020952180626
46814CB00003B/1050